D1806582

THE JACKPORT KILLER

A VIRULENT NOIR

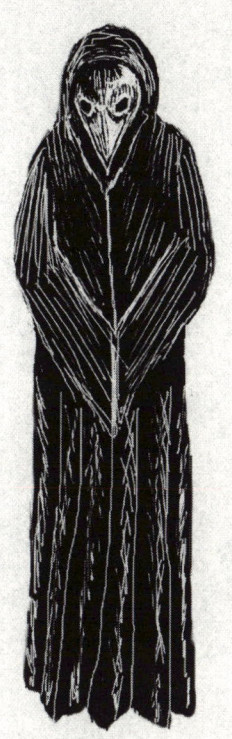

a Kurt Lobo Casefile

by KNEEL DOWNE

THE JACKPORT KILLER:

A Virulent Noir

A Kurt Lobo Casefile by KNEEL DOWNE

Copyright © 2014 by Kneel Downe

All rights reserved. This book or any portion thereof may not be reproduced or used in any manner whatsoever without the express written permission of the publisher except for the use of brief quotations in a book review or scholarly journal.

First Printing: 2014

ISBN 978-1-291-89063-1

www.VirulentBlurb.com

For James Knight...
The BAD BAD Poet.

An inspiration.

A peer.

And a valued friend.

Into The CITY we go...

Into The Deep

DARK

NEON WOODS...

Introductions

The WOLF is here...

Welcome to the first of The KURT LOBO CASEFILES, a series of short novels that explore the life and times of Detective Lobo before the events of VIRULENTBLURB:FRACTURES.

As is usual with my work, it began life as a Twitter Feed and was completed later in my subterranean bunker located just to the left of The Veil.

You will notice a particular style in the layout. Large gaps. Pauses. Far too many ....

This is intentional.

The Wolf has a certain 'Beat' to his stories and speech.

Much is said and inferred in these gaps. Go with it. Soon you will understand.

If you are a new reader Welcome! And I hope you are inspired to venture further into The Virulent Blurb Universe.

For regular readers...Hello there, thanks for coming back. I have sprinkled various cameos and hints throughout the book just for you.

And for the real Blurb Historians...This case takes place exactly Twelve Months before the events in FRACTURES.

As usual I need to thank Steven and Susan for being the backbone of my rapidly expanding Universe...this one's for you Kids.

Well...that's enough from me. The Wolf is waiting for you.
Please enjoy.

KNEEL DOWNE May 2014.
Somewhere inside The Veil.

BEGINNINGS...

Is this fucking thing on?

Testing. Testing? I hate technology.....technology and Poets....

Fuckers always mess with your head.....

Keep a journal, they said....keep track of your thoughts, Kurt....
At my age you don't wanna keep anything....
Fuckers.

Shit....

Lobo. Kurt. Detective in this dusty old whore we call the City.

Home.

Audio Feed Alpha initiated.....

4.35am when I get the call....
I'm still knocking back the Vodkacaine and thinking about sleep....

Think again old Wolf...

I find my WristCom in the dark...fucking power's out again....it's Gordon.
All he says is...

"He's struck again, Kurt."

I shudder...

Takes me five minutes to locate my boots and hat....

Turns out I'm still wearing them.

Good start Kurt....

My bones do that thing as I stumble to the door...the bad thing.
I swallow a curse along with my ReGen pill....

Both taste like shit....
Hallway's a nightmare of flickering emergency lighting....spins my head.

I smell heavy jasmine and cinnamon....

A figure rushes by...

It's that girl again....
Seen her a lot recently...in the shadows....guess she must have just moved in...

Something kinda weird about her...

"God speed Detective." She whispers and before I can dredge up a snappy Lobo response, she's gone....

Just her scent remains....

Leave the car where it is...the crime scene's only a block away...the streets are empty...just wandering ads and the dust.

Me and the dust.

I remember back to the day the Sun and Stars vanished....

Fuck me....we thought it was snowing...

Fucking snowing....

The whole building's dark....seems the backup generator's out....

There's a Rhino spliced cop at the door...can't find his name...
Greets me

"Kurt...we didn't touch a thing...watch your step chief....the stairs are kinda old."

I throw him a nod and a grunt...he catches them...

Fuck me but he was right....whole damn building's older than me.... smells the same too...

Deserted except for small scurrying things....

I keep my LuminoGlobe dead.....find my way with my nose...heavy blood stench...

The only light from my cigar...

Soft red glow....

Find the room....

The floor crunches with broken glass....my boots sliding and slipping and then...

And then....

Then the power kicks in...

Momentary blindness....

My eyes adjust and...

Fuck me.....

Oh dear lord fuck me......

It sure as hell ain't glass....

The floor's covered in eyes...

Droid eyes...

Must be thousands of them....

And there, centre fucking stage....

Strung on tubes and wires from the ceiling....

Some kinda twisted cruel cruciform....

A young woman...deer spliced....

Silver steel rod rammed behind the right ear...

Naked.

Used....

And...

Fuck me....

Across the breasts....a message....

Carved into pure soft fur....

A fucking message....

"HELLO KURT"

The blood's already congealed.....

My stomach does a thing....

A bad thing.

I swallow it.

There's no doubt about it...none.

The JACKPORT KILLER is back....

I take a moment...no, scrub that...I take a fucking handful....my name mocks me in blood...

Don't look in the eyes old man...

I look...

I make a noise...pause....make it again.

Break a gaze and punch my WristCom....

It does that musical shit...
"Gordon? It's Kurt..."

"Wake the kid up and get the Mouse up to speed.....I need them both down here....

Oh, and Gordon? Call the Witch...I'm gonna need her."

I hear him gasp....Gordon gives good gasp....

"The feckin Witch?
But you hardly see eye to eye Kurt!

Are you sure about this?"

I become grunt...
Grunt becomes me...

"I won't fucking bite...I promise...
This one's fresher than the others.....

She might find something."

The call kisses termination and the silence returns...

Just the squeak and groan of crucified wire as the bloodied doe swings gently...

Get to work old man...

Make myself move...

The window is broken...shards of plexi glass...

A pile of drifting dust and yes...

An imprint

Ha!
A cloven hoof? A cloven fucking hoof?

You gotta do better than that you fucker....

This Wolf doesn't believe in any Voodoo shit...
Catches my eye...

Words scratched into ancient plaster...

I crouch low and my back does that cursing thing...

Breathe deep and ignore it.

'WELCOME TO THE LODGE'

The fuck does that mean?!?
I fish for my data pad.....pockets full of ancient crap...

Make some notes...

Lower down...

Tiny fucking script...

Upside down and scrawled in blood...

One single hateful word....

'KATRINA'

Like a kick in the fucking guts.......

49 years and the wound still fucking screams...

I catch my breath...

Fumble and drop it...

It falls without a fucking sound...

This bastard knows me....done their fucking research...

Made it personal....

Fine by me you sick fuck...

Bring it on...

I do the standing up thing....wish I hadn't....

My spine pops and I'm dancing with coloured stars...

Wait for it to clear...

A sound?

BUZZING?

Feel my ears do that twitch...

There, around the JackPort....

Vortex Flies crawling...

Sucking crimson...

Eating and fucking on something long dead....

If I did metaphors, and I don't, I'd say that sums up our whole damn city...

Nails us all...

I'm not touching anything....that's Dorian's job...

Me?

I just look and smell...

But my nose finds nothing...

Again.

I check behind the ear...

Already knowing what I'll find...

23 inches of polished surgical steel....
Rammed deep into the port.

Part of the ear has come away...

I figure she must have fought back right to the ugly fucking end...

I fall in love with her a little...

Move round the front...

My boots crunch another few blind Droid eyes...

More splinters to clean up...

Something new...

The mouth partly open...

Something plastic and clear protruding...

I reach for my tweezers....

Tease it out through Mortis jaws...

Antique newsprint sealed in laminate...

A headline I know all too well...

Shit.

'ACCLAIMED DETECTIVE'S WIFE KILLED IN SKIN REAPER ENQUIRY'

I'm gonna find you.....you bastard....

Place it in an evidence pod....

Turn my attention to the soft furred chest...

Deep letters slashed...

Nipples removed...

Lower.

I recognize the ugly familiar ruin where something beautiful once dwelt...

Brutal painful cutting....

I know what caused it....

What we will find....

Inserted exactly 17 inches inside....

A shard of mirror.....

Painted jet black.

The last two victims were male....

Now there's a fucking image to play with....

No, don't thank me....I'm generous that way.

I bend my head and inhale....

But nothing...not a thing.

Just Terror's final piss and the onset of the rot....

And that's how the Witch finds me....

Snout deep in a dead girl's crotch....

Smooth Kurt.....fucking smooth...

"Always the romantic, Detective..."

I bite my tongue....

No, really I do....

Iron floods my mouth...

I ignore my back and make a point of straightening up easily...

Pull on my cigar...

Turn and nod.

My body calls me a bad name...

"Sanderson"

I'm playing nice....trying to remember the rules of that game....

Pretty sure punching someone out isn't one of them...

Never got on with the Witches....something about them puts me on edge...

Oh, and we're not supposed to call them Witches anymore...manners?

Take a look at Sanderson of the Psych Division then....

It's like someone stuffed a melodramatic Crow into a leather catsuit....

And a cloak....

Fuckers always wear a cloak....

Fuck me sideways and call me a cab.

She's giving me that look...

The shit on my boots look...

I decline it and plough straight in...

"You getting anything?"

The raised hand...

Demanding silence...

Who teaches these fuckers that kinda shit anyway?

She turns on her pretty little heels...muttering

"Trauma....intense painful trauma."

I nearly choke on a response...

Comes out as a lame ass bark...

Trauma? No fucking shit...

Now it's fingers to the temple time...

Bowed head...

And you wonder why these jokers wind me up?

Her lips are moving....whispering...

"When he used her....it was cold....

FREEZING....

Like ice...."

She throws me another look...

This time I catch it...

Wish I hadn't...

It has the stench of terror all over it....

"She never saw him....

Not once...

Not even as he was

As he...

As he violated her...."

That word, like a slap to my face...

The fuck is this?!?

"So we've got an invisible killer who also has no scent and not even a trace of DNA?

Is that what you're saying?"

I'm harsh...

Too harsh...

Rein it in old man...

Let her do her voodoo.

I make a placating gesture...
Feels odd...out of place...

"I need time...time...I need....alone."

She's doing that shaking thing...

Part of me feels sorry for her.

I ignore it.

"Take as much as you like kid...I'll be out in the hallway..."

She's zoned out...off in fairy land...doesn't hear me.

I do a leave...

I lean against the doorframe...

Swallow some smoke...

Something with too many legs and eyes falls onto my arm...

Crawls...

I crush it.

Jesus!!

I wish I hadn't...

Hands a stain of purple goo and that fucking stench...

What the hell kinda bugs are we living with these days?

Now the lights are on I can see just how fucked this building is...

Scuff marks in the dust...

Figure he dragged her up each painful step.

What's that?

Something stuck in the banister's base....

Sharp and bloodied...

A finger nail?

Fuck.

She was conscious you bastard......

I sniff around but there's nothing....

Just the girl...

The fear...

And that shitty stench of dust and rot....

DeadBox, Kurt? I can hear you asking...

Why not just use a DeadBox and ask the victims themselves?

Smart little fuckers ain't you?

We tried....

Hell, not me...

I hate the fucking things but believe me....

We tried....

Nothing.

Whatever this invisible, scentless bastard does to them, they stay hidden...

Wiped out completely...

Is that possible?

Something cold sneaks into my bones....

Sticks around...

A shiver?

Fuck me but I feel old...

Too old.

Footsteps distract me...

Must be the Kid and the Mouse...

About fucking time...we got a crime scene to sweep...

I turn and face...

Shit!

Samuel....

Sanderson's partner and all round creepy fuck....

He's wearing a cape with chrome stars at the collar...

Fuck me...

I cock a thumb towards the door...

"Your keeper's in there..."

Cold smile.

"My partner, detective."

I give the shrug....

"Whatever."

Odd....I usually get along with Dog Splices but this guy...

He's Doberman spliced and just all kinda wrongs...

Kinda effeminate...

Like some sorta broken ballet dancer...

Precise but splintered....

Don't get me wrong....

I don't care who or what you wanna fuck...

I'd be more than happy if you all went and fucked yourselves...

But this guy...

All wrong...

And he's got those crazy cracked eyes...

You know the ones? Like shattered glass?

Yeah, those...

He's gone...

Just his heavy stink remains...

Gonna take me hours to get his fucking musk outta my damn nose...

"Kurt?"

At last...quick foot falls ....

Meet my partner....

Good guy but he's a Rat...

No....really his is...

Officer Geldof....

Shiny black leather...

Gleaming cop badge...

Twitching nose...

I figure he's about 48 now....

Fucker still looks 14.

I give him the greet...

"Kid."

Do some pointing...

"Bastard's left us a whole lotta badness..."

He nods.

He gives good nod...

"Dorian's on his way up... collecting his stuff."
I grunt.

This is good...Dorian's the best Forensic in this whole dump.

He's also a Mouse.

I do a turn...

Re enter the room...

"Knock fucking knock."

(Hell, it makes me smile)

"The Spirit World given us anything yet?"

The Dog ignores me....

Sanderson wafts over....

She ain't looking too good....

Drained.

Got a red eyed shake going on....

A sigh...

"He kept her elsewhere.....

Brought her here at the very end....

For the spectacle..."

I make my knowledgeable noise....

Sounds like I've got gas...

Do a squint...

"That's his usual M.O."

She won't catch my eyes....

Good job...

I didn't throw them.

Intimate ain't my thing, girl...I don't do intimate...

Just give me answers

"He used her...

Repeatedly....

All of her."

A pause...

Shit woman, I get your meaning....

"The coldness burned her....agony."

"That's it!?"

Damn old man....watch that gruffness.....

"Sorry....

You need time to think, Sanderson?

To process?"

Now she locks eyes...

And trust me, right then I would have done anything for a fucking key....

I see terror and hauntings...

"Yes....

I need to step back....

So....so much...

So much darkness...

Images I don't understand...

And words......."

I do a start...

Don't stop...

"Words?!.......

You heard this fucker?"

A nod.

A breakthrough?

Shit....no.

Shaken head....

"He was using a RemixBox....

At least I pray he was..."

Looks away.

"No one....

No thing, should ever sound like that..."

I'm being tugged...

And not in a good way.

There's a Mouse at my shoulder....holding a Body Scanner and doing that flustered thing...

"Mouse."

"Kurt....I've got some readings....."

Pushes those wire framed glasses back up the bridge of his nose...

I make the expectant face....

"Um, er, yes....there's significant ReGen in her blood stream....

A reduced dose of course but still...."

I give a growl....

"He kept her alive and repairing as long as he could?"

Oh you bastard....

You're gonna pay for all this....

"Um, yes.....

It seems he wanted her to experience everything....

Right to the...er,

Er...to the very end...."

Another growl...

Pull yourself together Kurt....

This is what the fucker wants.....

Hold on....the Mouse is still speaking....

"Whoah.....

Backtrack Mouse....

What you saying?"

He gives me some good exasperation....

Continues...

"The scan showed something else Kurt....

Placed further in than the mirror shard....

Something metallic....

Do we?"

Another new factor.....

The fucker's playing with us...

Leading us a twisted fucking dance....

I do the thinking...

Metallic?

Could be anything....

Could be viable...

Dangerous?

I weigh some odds...

The Precinct or here?

"Remove it here....

Lower risk of collateral damage....

And Mouse....Dorian"

"Kurt?"

"Be careful Mouse....

Fucking careful."

The Kid's taking image grabs....

Dog's staring blankly at the far wall...

Dust drifts the window.

Time does its thing and then Sanderson

Still shaking....

"Tell me Detective.....

Have you ever heard the legend of the Lodge?"

Behind me I hear the unpleasant suction of removed mirror....buzz of flies...

I give her my quizzical face...

It suits me...

"Shoot kid...."

She's taking that big breath....

"Certain old texts speak of a place...

A door...

A gateway if you like..."

She's rocking that far away look...

I figure what the hell....

But then...

Behind me....

The tinkle of metal on concrete....

And god save me....

My body knows....

Right there and then....

Fuck me.....it knows....

I do the turn....

The Kid and the Mouse....

Inspecting something....

The Kid looks at me....

Fearful....

Don't remember moving but I'm there...

Pushing aside....

Reaching for that object....

Glitters of gold....

The kid says,

"BOSS!"

But I'm gone....

I'm gazing at something impossible....

A band of gold...

A fucking ring...

A wedding ring....

Seems to me its twin screams.....

Right here on my own fucking finger.....

I read the inscription.....
'FOR MY FLAME. LOVE, KURT'

Kat????

I feel the Wolf break free.....

I become Rage....

The Howl....

The Kid goes flying....

Sprawling....

I'm anger's fucking body and I'm burning.....

Fingers in my mind....

Warm.

Soothing.

The Witch....

Sanderson...

I'm outside....

Gasping.

Crying?

"Detective....Kurt.....go home...now!

We will deal with this....we will take the greatest care of it....

Of her...."

She takes the ring....

My hands don't resist...

Her fucking blanket still in my head....

My mind....

Passes the time....

I'm cold....

I'm myself again...

My apartment....

The dirty, sick bastard has been in my home and I didn't even notice....

But worse...

Worse...

I didn't even know it was missing....

Must be two weeks since I last checked.....

Stupid old man....

Kat....

Katrina....

I'm sorry....

So fucking sorry...

I haven't forgotten, my love.....

I dig my pockets...

Evidence from an old raid...

Locate them...

Two blue capsules....

Covered in fluff and grit....

I snap the Stimms open and suck oblivion up my stupid fucking old snout....

The day turns to static....
Goes away.....

Three hours later and I'm down by the docks....

Holding onto the railings....

There's a quart of Vodkacaine in my hand...

Bad taste mouth

Someone's howling....

Long and mournful...

Fuck this shit....

It's me.

I do a stop.

I cease and desist.

Slipshod flashes of shifting Neon and snarling rage...

Thrown fists?

The last few hours have gone...

Colour me fucking glad...

This is the place I said goodbye to her...

To reason and hope....

To Katrina.

Just ashes on thick oiled water...

Falling like dust.

My body does a thing...

A coughing thing.

Heaving....

I retch and become vomit....

Truth is.....it seems kinda apt...

I do a spit....

Do some more...

Straighten up and wipe my snout.

Something crusted yellow slips from my nose...

Falls into the water.

Fuck this!!

Shape up old man...

The bottle's at mouth before I think about it....

That comfortable fucking burn...

My eyes leak...

Check my head....

Yeah, hat still in place....

Cigar still wedged in my mouth....

What can I say?

I'm a fucking professional.....

The world swims....

Swims back again....

Lungs of smoke and an electric ember glow.....

I'm coming back to myself...

Not quick enough it seems.....

I don't even hear them approach.....

Sloppy Kurt.

Sloppy......

A hand on my arm....

Without thinking I'm swirling....

Grabbing the sneaky fuck...

BoltGun pressed against another's head...

Twitchy.

Soft cinnamon hair...

Wrap around VizShades...

Leather jacket.

Long and battered.

Knowing smile.

It's the girl from my building...

"Are you lost Detective?"

I lower the gun....smell it's oil.

Holster it.

Unsure how to play this...

I go for gruff....it's my default...

"You got some nerve kid....most people would have pissed themselves."

Again the smile.

"Oh, I've never been afraid of the big bad Wolf."

Silence does its thing....

Sticks around.

I zone back in...

Her lips are moving....

"I said are you lost poor Mr Wolf?
Are you far from home?"

The fuck?

"I'm on a case kid...I'm working."

I stink of vomit and booze....

I'm pretty sure she knows what I've been working on....

Forgetfulness...

Now she's at my side...

I'm still jumping moments.

God damn fucking Stimms....

She's gazing at the water.

Her perfume surrounds me...

"We all find ourselves lost sometimes Detective....

We're all a long way from home..."

I catch a bad word.

Swallow it.

Fuck me.....

She's at my ear....

Whispering....

Some kinda new age shit?

What?

"The Lodge has many doors my sweet Wolf.....but only two possible exits...

Do you understand?

Do you remember?"

Her perfume is messing with me more than the Stimms....

I feel a forgotten hardness.

I do that shaking head thing.

Wish I hadn't.....

"Look, kid?"

Interrupts me...

"Even in the dark we can find our way, little Wolf...

We can find our deliverance....."

"Seriously kid.....who the flying fuck are you?"

Tinkling broken glass laughter...

"Today you can call me Emily....but it isn't my name."

My WristCom does its noisy shit....

It's Geldof checking on me...

I swear I'm fine.

Don't apologize....

He wouldn't expect me to...

Turn back and she's gone...

Just cinnamon, me and the dirty fucking water...

All three of us are rippling...

I do a walk...

Do some more.

Pound some fucking streets.

Think some things.

Kurt is back...

Still angry but now with added coldness...

It's my Block....

My dirty fucking Block....

Some sorta home I guess...

I hear the screaming before I open the doors....

Take the stairs like a much younger Wolf...three at a time...

For once my body plays along.... Fifth floor.

My floor.

A screaming woman.

It's Rabbit Girl from down the hall....

She's doing that shake and pointing....

Pointing at a door.

My fucking door.....

I don't even pause....

I'm back in the zone...

Cylinders firing....

My door...stained with red...

Ajar and sporting a new decoration....

Fuck me!

A head....

A FoxBoy by the look of it....

Telltale silver spike behind the ear....

Another longer one pins it to the door...

Entry point between the eyes...

The third eye? This sick fuck has a thing for mystic shit...

Must a taken some strength to do this....

I don't wanna look but I do...

Yeah, there beneath the trailing blood....

Something else new.

Rammed where the eyes should be...

Two brass JackPorts....

Gleaming...

Looks like the eyeballs musta popped....

There's opaque shit all over the floor....

Something black...

Forced between the lips...

A VoiceBox....

A kid's toy...all plastic and mesh...

More blood dripping...

Good...fresh.

It's set on proximity alert...

Room fucking guard mode...

Starts singing as I approach...

"WELCOME HOME KURT....WELCOME HOME KURT...WEL"

Heavily phazed and distorted...

We won't trace anything from it...

I do an ignore and cautiously push my door....

It swings like a pro

Yeah yeah....I hear you all shouting...

'Procedure Kurt!'

Bullshit....the guy's not booby trapped anything...

He wants me to see this...

The place is a fucking mess...

But it's my mess.

Overhead phosfors are on...

I smell the addition before I see it...

Heavy copper blood

There....

Scrawled above Kat's HoloFrame...

In lurid drying red...

CATCH ME CATCH ME IF YOU CAN......

OK...game on fucker.

I find the rest of FoxBoy in my bed...

Right hand missing.

Left hand has the two middle fingers removed...

Poor fucker looks comfy...

I locate the hand on my bedside table....

Clutching my service commendments....

Fuck knows where the fingers are...

But there's more....

Judging by the splattered red on my sheets...

Crotch level...

Something else must be missing...

I figure I won't check my fridge...

I do a breath...

Figure what the fuck and do another..

Step back old Wolf....don't let the sick fuck play you.

I do a leave...call it in.

Something new this time though...

Not so clever are you, you bastard?

A scent.... Faint but a scent...

Like something electrical...
New.

I try to name it....

Fail.

Leave it to fester and grow...

I do a leave....

Let the boys deal with this one...

For now....

Three doors down the hall...

BadgerLady...

I knock.

"Val? I need to use your shower."

She doesn't even blink...

She's good people...

A bottle tells me I'm using BadgerShine...
Why the fuck not? Water plays my scars...

Revives me.

So many scars.

I hear the sirens arrive

I stay in the shower until the dark, black puddles are finally washed away....
Got the water way too hot...

Remember to shower more old man.

Step from the cubicle...

Old cracked claws clicking on Poly Vinyl flooring...

A comforting sound...

Grab a towel...

Ignore the mirror...

Val's thrown my clothes in the CleanBox....

They sit waiting for me in a neatly folded pile...

I can smell white musk and Foramix....

I do a dress....

I'm all edges and careful creases...

Fuck me but it takes me back....

Back to days of order and calm and soft, soft fur.

Something hot and meaty waits for me in the other room...

I pick up the mug and take a sip...

Check the note...
'TRY NOT TO BREAK ANYTHING'

I make with the smile...

Time was, me and Kat would babysit for Val...

Nice kid...

I've forgotten his name...

Military guy now, I think...

Image files above the fireplace...

Kat smiles at me...

I open up a little...

Twinge in the chest...

Yeah, still working I guess....

Make with a yawn...

Locate my hat and coat...

Heavy old stench...cigars and sweat.

She knows better than that...

No one cleans my coat...

Outside the apartment I hear someone doing a vomit...

Figure one of the Rookies must have looked in the fridge...

Maybe I smile...

I finally relent and check the MirrorCam....

Kinda clean, kinda sharp...

Too much grey around my snout...

I say a bad word...

Sounds good.

Place the mug in the sink...

Kill the overhead phosfors...

Make a mental note to buy Val some wine...

Make the door do its thing...

I step into fucking mayhem...

Corridor's full of cops, body pods and maintaining Meks...

My apartment bathed in Crime Scene beams....

The kid sees me...

Does that rushing over thing...

Gives me the eye...

If he mentions my cleanliness I swear I'll deck him....

"Kurt? You've had a...."

"Leave it kid....don't go there..."

He makes with the hurt face...

He gives good hurt...

I stride past him...

I indicate my door...

Make with the quizzical...

"Speak to me kid."

I see him swallow some commiserations....

He knows me too well...

"Dorian's just finishing up....he wants to see you. Something new."

I do the nod...

Fire up my smoke...

"OK kid....let's do this..."

Samuel's at my door...

Staring at FoxBoy like some kinda twisted fucking mirror.

I make some words...

"Figured you'd be wafting around..."

He doesn't look at me...

Gives a melodramatic grimace....

"The smell in there was distasteful to me Detective...."

I snort a snort...

"Thought you guys would be used to the stench of death?"

He makes with the turn...

Gives me the eye...

The cold one...

"I was referring to the stink of Wolf..."

Hint of a smile...

I let it ride...

Way too soon to get my clean clothes blood stained....

The Crime Scene beams play across my coat as I enter...

Yellow and Black.

Dorian and the Witch are in the corner doing that heated talking

The Mouse sees me...

Makes with the beckon.

I become beckoned...

"You must tell him!" Hisses the Witch...

Paint me intrigued....

"Tell me what?"

Dorian's got the flustered on...

It suits him.

Sighs.

"Kurt...Sanderson's got a rather interesting yet esoteric theory."

She shoots him that look only women can do...

Snaps...

"You ran the checks! The results back me up..."

Mouse gives a shrug...

I wait...

"Tell me." She says. "Have you heard of the Etheric Field, Detective?"

I play dumb...

It's a song I know all the lyrics to.

"Humour me?"

"Joshua Knight discovered the existence of the field...we all have one...It's how all his inventions work. DreamCages, Noonian Spheres...."

I let her talk...

I know all this New Age bullshit but I want her take on it...

I need an avenue...

Need me some clues....

"Even DeadBoxes....

It's the engine of our dreaming..."

Gives a pause.

"Knight even hinted it may be the numerical proof of our soul."

I make with the dismissive...

"Sounds like the kinda batshit crap he would come out with..."

I enjoy her outrage...

It tastes good...

She's a little red...

"Joshua Knight was the father of our New Age....

A genius!!"

Yeah, yeah....same old same...50 years of this shit...

"He may be a father to you, lady....

But to me he was always just another crazy Mother...."

I let the last word go AWOL...

We do a glower....

Dorian pipes up...

"Er...Kurt, at Sanderson's insistence I ran an Etheric test...."

OK....

Now I'm giving a shit....

"And?"

He's blending flustered and embarrassed... Checks his pad...

"Not a trace Kurt....the entire Etheric Field has been removed....."

I let the information sink....

Drag me some smoke...

I know where this is going....

I don't like it but it makes some kinda sense....

"It would explain why we can't find them in the DeadSpace." Says the Witch....

"Why I can't hear them well...."

I get a cold shiver....

I give a sigh...

I give good sigh....

"So this Fuck is invisible... No scent...he rapes, tortures and abuses his victims..."

"And now you're trying to tell me after all that, he steals their souls?"

I'm watching the Witch...

She never flinches...

I plough on...

"And to top it all off he appears to have some kinda raging hard on over me.....is that what we've got here?"

Geldof speaks up...

His whiskers doing that twitch...

"Looks that way Chief."

He's a good kid....

Always cuts through the shit....

I swallow some smoke....

Give it my best Lobo...

The old one...

"Fair enough....

I've seen worse...

Let's go catch this fucker..."

A splintering noise breaks the moment...

I guess FoxBoy has been removed from my door...

Someone curses.
I don't bother looking....

"We can get you a new door Kurt...."

The Mouse is apologetic...

Hear myself making a snarl.

"Leave it as it is!

Just fucking leave it."

Something heavy and hydrological enters the room...

A Maintaining Mek...

Geldof gives me a look...

"We'll make sure the place is cleaned."

I go pocket fishing...

Find what I'm after...

Smooth and circuit deadly...toss it to the Mouse...

"Make sure you set this up Dorian."

Geldof is with that face....

The shocked one...

"But Kurt.....that's illegal...."

I spin round...

Give him some noise...

"I'm a cop kid....Nothing I do is illegal...got that?

I want this place Daisy Chained...

Anyone but me comes in here?
Diced fucking meat."

Dorian pockets the device...

"I'll get on it Kurt....is it...?"

Questioning.

"Yeah...it's fixed to my gene code...set the fucker to Ultra."

One last glance round the room then I motion to the kid...

Mek oil in my nose...

Time to leave...

Got me some thoughts to start thinking.

"C'mon kid...we got things to do..."

Dorian's wandered away already.

Directing the Rookies with the Body Pods.

One has vomit on his suit.

The Witch grabs me at the door...

Slips something into my hand...

Something circular, smooth and gold...

"We cleaned it well." She says...

Fuck me but I could kiss her...

I settle for a cold, gruff

"Thanks...."

We share something like a smile...

I turn away...

Leave.

Samuel's still outside...

Crouching down...

Wearing that dumbass meditation face...

I give him a nod.

"Good luck dog...

Break a neck."

We take the lift...

I've seen enough fucking stairs today...

The kid's giving me a look...

I know exactly what he's gonna say...

A cough...

"Chief....Kurt?

You know there's an empty apartment next to me and Mary...

Why do you still live in this dump?"

Swallow some bad words.

Some anger...

He means well...

"It's my home kid...

It was OUR home...."

He does some silence...

The Dust has got heavier since my earlier adventures...

We dodge excited little Cleaning Meks on the way to the car...

I kick one, nicely.

Keep it smart and cool Kurt...

This guy knows you...

Your routine...

Knew just when you would get this morning's call...

Was waiting...

Knew how to sneak in unseen...

Sneak in and leave me a special fucking present in my own home...

But he broke his own M.O....

Sloppy....

I figure he's letting his own excitement and hatred take control of his actions...

Play it cold old Wolf...

Wait for the mistake...

We reach the car...

Someone has written a message on the windscreen...

In the dust....

Partly obscured by the fresh fall.

Still legible

'SUCH SWEET EXQUISITE PAIN.'

I figure it's been here thirty minutes at tops.....

The kid throws me a questioning look.

I catch it...

Some random lunatic or something more?

I let the kid catch some Image Grabs before I wipe it away...

This day is becoming fucked up central

The car's nearly as old as me...

A real gas guzzling antique...

I mean c'mon...

It still has fucking wheels...

I love my fucking car...

I pop the doors and throw the keys to the kid...

"You're driving kid...I'm over the limit."

He looks that look.

I take a swig to be sure.

We pull away....

He makes the tyres do that squeal...

I like that kinda shit...

And he knows it...

He's a good partner....

"Where we heading Boss?"

I let the question hang...

Do some window staring...

Watch me some neon and dust...

Always falling.

Always...

Something's in my head...

Whispering....

But just out of reach.

Something someone said....

Recently...

The fuck was it?

Then it hits me....

I make with a bark...

"Hang a left kid!"

We take the junction at speed...

Oh you clever, sneaky girl...I owe you...

"Boss?"

"When you're dealing with insanity, kid...what do you need to do?"

He gives me blank.

Impressive blank.....

I do a sigh....

"You go talk to the insane, kid....

Get the inside track...

Find your Deliverance....."

I watch comprehension hit him...

He gasps... "So we're?"

"Bingo kid...we're paying a visit to the Cascade...the Copper Fucking Cascade..."

A DARK INTERLUDE...

The place where madness lives...

We take the bridge over Thought and Redemption....

Hang a right onto Kafka and there it is...

Sitting on the hill like a haunted house...

Nowhere near as large as the Pyramid or Ellis Towers...

It's still an imposing fucking place...

Moonlight glinting on Copper panels...

Originally built to treat the victims of that major fuck up on the moon...

The Armstrong casualties...

These days it has stranger guests...

You ask me?

Everyone in this fucking city is insane.

But if you cross a certain line you end up here...

The fucking Asylum.

The Cascade.

'Course, these days everyone knows it as the place we stuck the vigilantes....

The spandex clowns...

The Super Fucking Heroes...

Technology?

Poets?

Lion Splicers?

The things I hate....

You can add Super Heroes to the top of that fucking list...

Fucking dicks.

They appeared a few years before the Fall....

No one knows where the fuckers came from...

They just arrived...

Overnight fucking sensation

Truthfully?

At first they were kinda useful...

Kinda impressive...

I even worked with a few.

At first....

You know this place...

This City...

It's always been full of whack jobs that need taking down...

Dangerous fucks...

They served a purpose

Trouble was...

After a few years of apprehending bad guys they upped the stakes...

Formed a team and changed the rules...

Lost the gloves

The team?

Fuck me...

You surely can't have forgotten the VENGEFUL SQUAD?

The decade of fucking mayhem that followed...

The destruction?

Soon there were no more Bad Guys to catch....

Why?

Because these Nut jobs had killed them all...

It was a fucking slaughter...

So we rounded them up...

Stuck them in here...

Everything in this City runs out of usefulness....

Remember that Kurt...

Remember that...

We pull into the driveway...

The kid does a shiver...

He hates this place.

Can't say I blame him...

I figure I'll leave him in the car.

Some guy steps out in front of us...

All raised hands and weapons...

Geldof hits the brakes.

I hit the dashboard...

I do a curse...

Great....

A new guy.

Jack Russell splice by the look of it.

Pristine uniform...

I can smell the fucking self importance from here...

Fuck this shit!

I pop the door...

Do an exit...

Ignore my back...

Make a growl...

Find a gun in my fucking face...

Now you see this?

This is gonna be fucking fun....

"I said show me your motherfucking pass!"

Guy's on some kinda power trip...

I can smell his sweat.

Figure he's been here a week...tops.

I make with the smile....

Feels more like a snarl...

In the car the kid's shaking his head...

Here goes...

"My pass?

Oh sorry...I think I left it....here!"

One fist says hello to his gut...

The other slaps his face...

Grabs the pistol.

I figure 'what the fuck' and grab his furry throat...

Do me some lifting...

Some holding...

He does a dangle...

Damn fine dangle....

"Now you see, Moonshine....

My pass is that you wouldn't have any inmates...

Any guests, if it wasn't for me...

And no fucking job..."

His eyes are giving good bulge....

I leave him hanging till I see the dark stain at his crotch...

Till I smell it...

Let the fucker fall...

"Ah, Kurt! I didn't know it was you..."

Brian steps from the gatehouse, swinging his pass.

"Oh, I see you've met the boy..."

We swap a smile...

They fit just fine...

He's a gnarly old bastard...

I've always liked him...

He swipes his card...punches some buttons.

"I'll let Doctor Nyman know you're on your way in....

You can park in lot 5...."

I make with the thanks...

Leave.

As I walk away I can hear him talking to the goon on the ground.

"Now then boy...are ye perhaps recalling that conversation about manners?"

Reach the door...

Do a standing...

Feel the security beam enter my iris...

Fuck me...

Still tickles after all this time...

Automated honey greets me...

"Welcome back Detective Lobo."

Hear the locks tumble and fall...

A beep or two...

The door does an open...

Step inside....

Familiar fucking stench...

Like polish and piss went on a date...

Do a cough...

Take the left hand corridor...

Nyman's waiting for me outside his office...

All smiles and handshakes...

He's sporting one of those generic mammal splices...

Money talks

"How can we help you today Detective Lobo?"

Forced joy...

He's like a cloud of goodwill, aftershave and light musk...

And despair.

I make with the greetings...

Press some pampered palm...

"I'm on a case Doctor...I need some insight...

I need to talk to him...."

A little fuck of a flicker gifts his eyes....

Gone...

A professional guy.....

"Why of course...

He's where he always is...."

He shuffles a shuffle...

"I'll let Barney know you're on your way up.... I take it you don't need a guard?"

I grunt.

"No....no guards."

I take a walk....

Know this shithole like the back of my paw...

Figure I'll take the stairs...

Give myself a little time...

Some courage

Stairwell Alpha....

From the basement I hear the groaning...

The never ending roar...

The rage.

That's where they keep Professor Green...

Three floors up and I bump into PHOTON and four guards....

The poor fuckers glad to see me...

Smiles at me...

For fuck's sake...

"Detective Lobo!
How goes the war against crime sir?"

The inhibitors at his neck and wrists do that flashing shit...

Flashing red...

"Going well Captain....

Going well..."

He gives me that look....

The pleading one...

"Have you come to release me, sir?"

Oh fuck....

Something hard in my throat...

Something forgotten...

I ignore it.

"I'm working on it Captain...just hang tight and...

Be vigilant, OK?"

Floor six....

This is where they keep SONIC SHRIEK and THE CREEPER....

I keep climbing...

Got no time for fucking house calls.....

Floor Nine...I change my mind...

Take a detour...

Wander a corridor until...

Bars.

Wide open space...

Walls covered in crude paintings...

Paintings of balloons...

A model circus...

The boy notices me.

Makes with the standing up thing...

"Detective!"

I smile...

"Hey PLUTO."

"You doing OK, kid?"

He's all flushed and excited....

"I'm bored sir....I'm waiting for our next mission..."

I feel like a cheap old shit.

"Soon enough, kid...

Soon enough..."

I turn away...

"Keep frosty kid...

Keep safe...."

I hear him call after me...

"Detective? Please....I haven't heard from my brother in months. I miss him."

"I'm on it kid....I'm on it."

Poor fuck never had a brother...

Pass floor twelve...

My left side does that pain...

Old scar complaining...

Fuck me but THE SHARP BLADE was a bastard to capture....

Reach my destination....

Barney's waiting for me.

We do a smile...

Looks me up and down...

"You know the drill Detective......"

"Sure do Barney......"

Shuffle my old ass in front of the metal cage...

Make with the waiting...

CLUNK....

Slowly opens...

Like a mouth.

"Good luck Mr Lobo...

He's been waiting for you...."

Of course he fucking has....

Doesn't surprise me...

Not a jot...

Steel door...

I catch a breath...

Kinda need them so I catch some more...

Time to meet madness...

Time to meet DARK DELIVERANCE.....

Swings the door...

No lights...

That voice...

That deep unsettling fucking voice....

"Good day Detective......you're two hours late..."

The lights kick in...

Afterburn in my eyes.

Picture this...

Stone and Copper plated walls....

A window...bars...

A bed and a chair.

A man.

Fuck me, I think he's a man...

Cross legged on the bed.

He's got that stillness thing going on...

Total studied stillness...

Body encased in something that resembles Black Leather...

I say resembles...

Whatever that shit is it's stronger than fucking steel.

Ridged gauntlets....

Body shielding...

Flowing cape. Yeah, I know....

A fucking cape!

And then there's that mask...

Like some kinda freaky fucking bird...

A Devil bird.

All edges and pointed to fuck.

But you wanna know the really whacked out thing?

That's not just a suit...

Not just a mask.

That shit is melded to his body in a way we don't understand....

That shit IS his body.

Cold intelligent eyes doing that thing...

"Tell me Detective, how was the boy?"

Throwing me a curve ball...

Testing me...

I catch it.

Toss that fucker straight back at him...

"The kid....Pluto, is fine...."

Pause...

"I thought you knew everything?"

Game on...

A smile.

Cold.

"I know that you spent 32 seconds talking to him and that your heart skipped three beats...

Regret perhaps?

"Guilt?"

We give it a moment...

Battle lines drawn.

We know each other well...

Go way back.

We understand each other...

Understand the dance...

Raised hand....

"Please Detective...

Take a seat.

I suspect your day has been a touch....

Stressful?"

His eyes never fucking blink...

I give it a sit...

Give it good sit.

My back thanks me.

He's watching me like some kinda cartoon fucking hawk...

Moves his lips...

"Tell me Lobo....

What did he add this time?

What did he leave for you to find?

To hurt you?

To bait you?"

I don't flinch...

Go straight ahead and tell him...

Every little thing.

We both value the truth...

Leave the bullshit for the other guys

He takes it all in...

Never makes a sound...

The lights are playing sliding games on his crazy fucking beak.

I finish.

Make with a wait

"So he knows you Detective?

He knows you well and for some reason he hates you....

Else why the second body?

Why the house call?"

I'm not fazed...

No...I don't know how but he hears everything....

Even stuck in here...

He knows everything that happens out there...

That's what he does...

What he is...

To tell you the truth he could break out of here anytime he wants...

I know it...

He knows it...

"Looks that way...

But for the life of me I can't figure who or why..."

I pause...

"Most people who hate me are fucking dead...."

That smile again....

"Dead....or in here Detective..."

I let it ride...

C'mon Deliverance...

C'mon you freaky bastard.
Give me something

Quicker than you know, the fucker is over by the window...

Stroking the bars...

I barely registered him moving...

Gazing at the dust...

"The rape, Detective...

The torture and abuse is not for pleasure...

Rather, it is a map...

A diagram...a code.

A quest for a door..."

I'm doing the mental notes...

Palms doing that sweaty slick shit...

He turns and gazes at me...

"What does he take from them, Lobo?"

I give him it all...

The Witch's theory...

The test results...

The whole fucking deal.

Passes a moment.

He nods slightly...

"So...

An invisible killer?

A stealer of souls?

Murders that follow the precision of a spell....

Tell me...are you battling magic, Wolf?"

A snort....

"I don't believe in that Voodoo shit Deliverance....

You know that!"

He laughs...

Fuck me, the fucker laughs...

"Indeed I do Detective....indeed I do.

But what if your killer does?

What then?

Tell me...what do you do then?"

There's a big old knot of angry in my throat...

Swallow it.

Breathe.

Carry on.

"You tell me .... You understand crazy...."

He ignores the jibe...

Keeps talking...

"Magic has many names, Lobo...you must discover the one name and find where it dwells..."

Another smile...

Almost a fucking grin...

"And you must watch your back Detective...watch your loved ones...

No one and nothing is safe."

Silence.

He's staring at me...

Head cocked...

I'm being dismissed...

Thank the fuck for that...

I need some fucking air...

I fish in my pocket...

Toss something to him...

A Data Chip...

It's caught and slotted into his wrist feed before you can say 'shit'...

"A gift Detective?

Why thank you..."

I do the Lobo grunt...

"13 months of unsolved crime...

Figured it would 'divert' you..."

"Yes...it may prove interesting...

Oh, Detective! I see you still haven't apprehended the Bad Poet?"

His face...

Mock sadness....

This time it's me smiling...

"You had forty years Moonbeam and neither did you...."

Game over...

Status Quo is regained...

It sticks in my throat...

Bitter...

But I manage a quick

"Thanks...."

Turn and wait for the door

His hand on my arm...

A vice...

Creepy fucking voice in my ear...

I consider going for my gun....

Not a fucking chance.

"One last thing Detective...

One last thing...

A message, if you will...

Left with me for you....

23 years ago...for this moment..."

"Left to you by a rather enigmatic young lady...

You may know her yourself....

If not, you will...

She has somewhat interesting eyes..."

"Tell him, she said...

Tell the old Wolf that this is just a skirmish....

Tell him the War is yet to come..."

"There is a storm coming Detective...

Maybe months away...

Maybe a year...

But it comes on Black Burning Wings...

Prepare yourself..."

And with that the fucker is back on his bed...

Eyes glazed over with the Data Flow...

I feel that coldness again...

Deep and bad...

Slams the door...

Barney is making with the banter...

But I'm gone...

Down those piss stenched stairs and out in the air.

In the dust...

ENDINGS…

Kid jumps as I open the door...

Sleepy fucker...

"Boss?"

"Not now kid....

Not now...

Just fucking drive OK?"

The streets and Neon stream by...

My head doing its stuff...

Make a decision....

"Drop me at the bar kid...I got some thoughts to kill."

The kid drops me a block away...

I figure the walk will do me good...

The streets are full of evening folk.

Questing for fuck knows what.

The Dust is getting heavier...

Worst I've seen it for years....swirling like a bad dream...

My vision's full of steaming grates and neon...

An automated Ad waddles past on stumpy little legs.
Little fucker's bleating about 'Big Joe's Gar Burgers'
Figure I'll give them a miss.

There's a DroidSplice crouched in a doorway....

Hair all wires and tubes...

He's stroking a MusicGlobe....

I stop and listen.

Old familiar tune.

One of Kat's favourites.

I let the notes float around me...

Sparkling motes of yellow and green...

I make memories...

The kid's good...

PlastiFlesh fingers teasing and caressing the sounds...

Fish in my pocket....

Throw him some loose credits...

And then it hits me...

My fur's on fucking end...

The play of a shiver...

Someone's watching me...

Following me?

Fingers do that flexing...

I feel my Sonic Baton fall into my old palm...

I make with a turn.

Nice and fucking slow....

Nothing.

No one.

Just me and the DroidSplice....

And the music.

Take a drag....

Casually check the windows and doors...

Take a breath old Wolf...

Step the fuck back...

Get a fucking grip....

The day's got me well and truly fucking spooked...

Nod to the musician and do myself some walking...

Still on edge...

Jumpy.

I can feel the drink calling out to me....

Like a lover...

Like a cheap fucking whore...

There's a commotion from one of the side streets ahead...

Some guy goes running...

Catch a flash and a scent of Zebra....

Then he's gone.

I hear it...

Smell it before I see it....

Deep rancid stench...

High pitched scratchy chattering...

That god awful hissing....

A fucking SpiderShade....

Kinda man shaped...

All legs and twisted bad news...

It drops from the alley wall...

Does a crouching....

This is what you get when you splice with a Spider...

A fucking nightmare...

They're the Pyramid's lap dogs...

Private security...

It gives me the once over....

Hisses a hiss...

The fuckers hate me...

With good reason.

The feeling's fucking mutual...

And then it's gone...

Scuttling off down the side street that ZebraBoy just ran down...

The fucker's hunting...

I feel sorry for the guy.

I turn away...

Nothing to do with me...

Not anymore...

The Pyramid's grown too fucking powerful recently...

Too fucking dangerous...

Make with the feet...

Pretend I don't hear a distant scream...

Brush some Dust from my sleeve...

Sometimes I hate this fucking city...

I can see the bar now...

Big old steel doors...

The RhinoSplice on the door...

Never bothered to know his name...

After all these years.

"Detective."

I produce a nod....

A smile.

Feels alien to me...

He returns both and pushes the door open for me...

I smell dry ice.

Welcome to THE FORGETTING ROOMS....

Best damn bar in this Dusty old shithole...

It's a maze of mirrors and liquid relief...

Sanctuary.

The D.J's a Walrus...

He throws me a wave...

Cranks the decks a little louder.

A bass line misses my face....

Bounces into a wall...

I watch it splinter into purple shards...

Fall and reform...

A new shape and sound...

I love me some fucking music...

Always have...

I remember older times....

Older songs....

I remember dancing....

It's not too packed tonight...

Still too early for the all nighters...

Just a mixture of the curious...returning from workers...the needy.

You can lay some fucking odds on which category I fall into....

Some days even I'm not fucking sure...

Not anymore...

The BarDroid has clocked me...

Already lining up the three glasses...

I throw him a curve ball...

"Gimme a beer as well....."

He inclines his head...

Freaky artificial smile...

"Good evening Mr Lobo....I trust you are well?"

Slides me the beer....

Fuck me but that tastes good....

Long and fucking cold...

I can feel it washing the dust from my throat....

From my mind.

Make with a finish.

Bang the glass down a little too heavy...

Grab me a short and neck it in one....

Bliss. The burn after the cold....

Wait.

Just for a moment.

Here it comes....

Old mother clarity...

The bastard buzz...

That pure fucking calm...

Some Medic guy once worked out how much I spend on booze...

Talked about my health...

I showed him some of my case files....

The bad ones

The little fucker never bothered me again...

I love it when a plan works out...

Take a look at the Bartender....

He's one of the high range Droids...

All PlastiFlesh and realism...

Unnerving.

The Elite Grade.

There's an obligatory ServoLock on his wrist...

All Droids are forced to wear them...

We both know it's a fake...

We don't talk about it.

People hate the Droids....

Fear them.

My opinion?

People are fucking dumb....

Me? I gotta lot of time for our mechanical cousins....

I've seen some shit in my time...

A whole load of shit.

But I've never seen a Droid act out of hatred...

No, it was compassion....

He's giving me the eye.

I fish in my pocket....

Locate what I'm after and repay the favour.

He catches it fluid and easy.

One of the eyes from the murder scene....

He holds it up to the light...

Turns it round.

Watches it gleam....

Never flinches.

"What do you make of that Pinocchio?"

He does that smile again...

I let him.

"It's an ocular unit 05.23 Detective...an antique...."

I make with a wait...

Let him continue...

"To tell you the truth I was under the impression they had all been recalled....destroyed."

"Why's that?"

"This unit was something of a failure Detective...

It has certain inherent flaws.

They caused certain problems..."

I do that carry on gesture...

He plays along.

"They were responsible for what people called Mechanical Religion....we saw things...."

We greet that silence shit....

Eventually he turns away...

Punches some buttons on the Bar's MirrorCam...

Lights do a flashing thing....

"Here....let me show you....I am now linked to the MirrorCam behind me....you will see what I see.....

Please give me a moment...."

He does something I wasn't really expecting to see...

Pops his fucking right eyeball out with his finger...

Places it on the bar...

Slides in the other...

There's a moment while the MirrorCam does that static shit....

And then I see myself sitting there...

You ask me? It looks pretty normal....

And then...
Slowly...

The picture becomes more colourful and a whole lot stranger....

It's the same scene but now everyone is surrounded by shifting fucking colours...

Pulsating...

Breathing...

Swirling....

The girl on the table behind me is bathed in a soft pink glow....

Flashes of blue and green...

Swimming around her....

Everywhere I look I see fucking colours...

Everyone has them....

So bright...

Take a look at myself....

Wish I fucking hadn't...

I'm a shroud of fucking red and black...

Streaks of purple....

All connected by some kinda shifting vortex behind my left ear....

"OK.......OK......

I get it...you can stop it now...."

He nods....

Turns to kill the feed...

But...

But....

But just before he does....

I swear I see a cloud of black and shining gold...

Sparks of radiant silver....

In the far corner....

I do a turn....a quick one...

There's no one there...

Feel that chill.

Get a fucking grip Lobo...

When I turn back the mirror is blank...

He rolls the eyeball back to me...

It sticks in a trail of spilt beer...

I knock back another short.

What the fuck?

Neck them both....

"The Lesser Droids believed we were witnessing the Soul Mr Lobo....

The proof of humanity's divinity...."

I make with a bark....

"And you? What did the fucking Elite figure you were seeing?

Fucking magic?"

He gives me that look...

The Droid one...

"No Detective....of course not.

Not magic....

The Etheric Field...

Science..."

BINGO!

I feel something click into place in my dusty old head...

But still just out of reach...

Come to me you fucker....

Wipe my jaw...

Swallow some smoke....

It's nearly there....

"Line them up again kid.....
Make them triples this time...."

Just finished the second....riding that burn....when I see something in the mirror...

The door...

Opening and closing...

But no one there.

I'm on my fucking feet before I know it...

Moving like a much younger Wolf...

No one fucking there!

That's when I get the call....

It's the kid...

I pause at the door...

Old paw on the handle...

He sounds kinda strange...

Emotional....

"Speak to me kid...Geldof?"

I hear me a gasp....

"Kurt....it's.....it's Mary...."

Something cold grabs my guts...

Something fucking cold

"Mary? Is she....."

"No, no Kurt...she's fine..."

My heart does that skip shit...

A sick relief travels my body...

"It's her office..."

"Her office?"

I let the gruffness back into my voice...

Slam those fucking walls back into place...

"The fuck's going on kid?"

He takes a moment....

I allow him two...and then the words come...

"It's him again Kurt....he got in here...left something...something bad."

I'm out onto the street and moving as the kid continues talking...

He's not focused...

Concern has made him sloppy...

I can get that...

"Where's Mary now kid?"

Nope, still babbling....

I give it a growl...
"Geldof! Where's Mary?!"

He finally makes with a pause....

"In the rest room Kurt...she's kinda shaken up..."

No shit?

"Listen kid...take her home...

Look after her....

I'll deal with this...."

"But Kurt....it's..."

I cut him off...

Whatever he wants to tell me is bad....

It can fucking wait till I get there....

That cold again.

"Take her home kid....

Love her...

I'll call you when I need you."

Terminate the call....turn back to the bar's doors.

Nod to Rhino boy.

"You see anyone leave here?
Just before I did?"

A leathery grunt...

"Nope....
Heard the door though...

It slammed once...."

I give him the quizzical...

He shrugs.
"Figured it was the wind..."

A snarl.

"When was the last time you felt wind, kid?"

He gives blank

I leave it...

Turn back to the task at hand...

Nose picks up that electrical smell again.

Burning?

Just a hint...

A trace.

How do you protect yourself against an invisible stalker?

A sick fucking killer?

Tell you the truth...

I'm fucked if I know....

Do some walking...

Cross me some streets...
Ignore some petty crimes...

Try to ignore my aching knees and fucked up guts...

Fail.

Mary works at OUR SISTERS OF HOPE...

The city's biggest hospital.

Clever kid.

Figure it'll take me twenty to get there...

Dust falls...

Take a detour by the DrugStore...

Flash my badge...

Buy me some drugs...

Crack the pod and inhale some coke...

Cold clarity drips...

Head's frozen...

Wait for the clouds to part...

Here we go....

Jump on board the sober fucking train...

The street gains edges...

Sharp.

On the corner of Faith and Despair some street Rat gives me the finger...impresses his friends.

Break his nose.

Keep walking.

It'll heal.

Brain's firing on all the cylinders it's still got...

I can feel things slotting into place...

Slowly.

It'll come to me soon...

There's a Hover crash on Faust...

Broken car...

Couple of bodies doing the ReGen jive....

Stains.

I nod to the Traffic cop...

Nearly there...

Stop for a moment...

Fish out my bottle....

Take a swig.

Drag some smoke...

I'm fucking primed....

Hear a noise....

Smell some oil.

Side street.

Some guy beating his Droid.

The Viral Lance buzzing and sparking in the shadows....

Shoot him in the kneecaps...

Call it in....main desk...

"Resisting arrest......twelve months minimum."

Bastard.

And I'm here....

Check my Chronometer...

Time's doing it's fucked up shit again...

I've arrived here ten minutes before I set out...

The kid's leading Mary down the steps.....

I blend into the shadows...

Ain't got time for feelings...

Not right now.

Watch them leave.

Take the steps...

Flashing lights.

Seems my whole life has been one big fucking flashing light...

An ambulance pulls up.

Doors play a bang symphony...

Some Stallion kid....

Neck wound.

He's bleeding out...

Fuck me he's gushing out...

A crimson fountain...

I know the signs...

Knife wound...

An Anti ReGen blade...

Yet another of the Pyramid's gifts...

Thank you fucking kindly....

Don't worry....

He'll live.

But that wound will never heal...

Poor fuck will be wearing a drip tray for the rest of his life....

And you wonder why I ain't got time for no poetry?

You still fucking wonder?

Busy foyer...
Some Dalmatian Girl puking in a bucket...

Two Ferret Cops...

Make to greet me...

Think better of it.

Smart guys....

The receptionist gives me those eyes.

The ones that tell you whatever's up there you don't wanna see it...

Not fucking ever....

Take the stairway....

Buy some time.

Break the second Coke Pod...

Guess I'm as ready as I ever will be....

Floor fucking five...

Mary's office has those fancy fucking sliding doors...

I know what's in there.

Who's in there...

I'm in his dirty fucking head now...

I'm starting to know you....

Understand you.

You sick fuck.

Waste some seconds watching the crime scene beams playing my coat...

Enter.

Sure enough....

Strung form the ceiling by Filament strands...

An inverted X shape...

Desk fucking dangling...

Dripping...

The familiar black and white hair...

Hanging down.

Body torn in so many fucking ways....

VAL....

I'm so sorry Val....

No....

I don't feel a thing.

No now...

That's for later...
For when the buzz has burnt itself out...

I think I make a crazy laugh...

I'm cold.

Automated...

A COP.

Walls daubed in words and symbols...

Blood and other fluids I figure...

So many this time....

I don't look at the stomach....

Not yet.

Not quite ready for that fucking treat...

There's something in the mouth...

Again....

Tweezers in my hand without thinking....

I'm an auto pilot of fucking procedure.....

Tease the object out.....

Fluid kisses my fingers...

A Key Card....

Plastic and snapped in half....

Bits of mouth....
Words.

"PROJECT AM"

The fuck is this?

Where's the other half?

Take a breath....

Do the math....

The CASCADE? The Bar?

About 4 hours....

Maybe 5?

You came straight here didn't you?

Straight here...

Val was a cleaner...old style work...

You knew her routine and you came straight here...

No need to stalk or capture this time...you bastard

So you came here and just waited.

No time to prepare.

No time for torture...

So how did you pass the time, you sick fuck?

How?

Not the messages on the fucking walls...

The scrawlings.

You needed her blood for that...

Her fluids.

Did you sit down?

Did you?

I bet the fuck you did........

I'm round the table quicker than my age or body suggests...

The chair is pulled to one side.

Unstained....

I bend low...

Ready...

Pass my snout over the PolyFabric...

No...

That's Mary.

I know that scent.

Sniff deeper old Wolf...

Deeper. Down.

Deep down...
There you are you bastard...

Still faint but there...

Electrical burning...

And something that smells like leaking battery cells...

I know this smell...

Can't figure why...

Not yet.

As I straighten up something coke and Vodka flavoured burns my throat...

Swallow it...

Something doesn't fit...

Think Kurt, think...

It's all there...

The steel rod behind the ear.

The ripping.

The fucking mayhem....

Think

Get me one of those waves...

The bad ones.

Seems the coke and Vodkacaine is wearing off...
Grab the table...

Hands slipping in Val...

Breathe you old fuck...

Breathe!

Whiteout's dancing when I notice the medicine cabinet...

Pray it's unlocked...

My luck's in...

Send some things sprawling...

Grab me some Adrenaline...

An Opiate Spike...

And, what the fuck?

Some pure medicinal grade Coke...

Do some self medication...

The Adrenaline first.

Like a fucking freight train...

Wash it down with some booze and the spike....

Fizzing.

Fuck me but the room's gained a fuckload of colour...

Edges and clarity...

Of course!
ReGen?

Val's fucking ReGen?

Despite the wounds she should be twitching like a Hendrix rider
who's fallen off the fucking Watchtower...

What gives?

Notice her bag...

Tossed to one side.

Open.

Smells of mints.

Musk.

And....

And it smells of Val...

Go digging...

Sifting...

Searching.

Not sure what I'm fucking after until it falls out...

Twirling into puddled gore.

A card...

White plastic.

One single blank 'P'...

Fuck me...

PURITY.

Val was a member?

How didn't I know?

Am I that fucking removed from life?

PURITY?

Yeah....those freaks.

The Natural Law loonies...

Turned their backs on ReGen use decades ago...

Old fashioned fucking mortals...

Can't figure if I'm angry or sad...

Figure what the fuck....

Let them meet halfway...

Settle for grateful...

At least she didn't suffer as long as the others did....

At least it would have been relatively quick...

Relatively....

Everything in this fucking twisted shithole is relative....

Right?

Got me too much clarity going on....
Noticing too many things.

Torn fur.

The hands.

Five deep slashes on each palm...

Applied salt?

Still ignoring the stomach...

Not yet for fuck's sake.

Not ready.

Turn my Adrenaline attention to the walls...

All those crazy words...

Some carved....

Sonic Blade?

Some daubed in blood...

And the others?

No, something much worse...

Don't need my nose to know that....

Symbols?

Snatches of words...

Whole sentences....

Things that look like fucking maps.
Owls?

Fucking Butterflies?

The moon....

More mentions of the Lodge....

Crude drawings of the Sun.

A Hawk headed guy?

Something about chairs...

And a girl?

Fucking skulls...

"They strapped us into metal chairs and invited them in."

"Skin like paper."

"The girl is not a girl....never was."

The fuck this means?

And then I notice something I recognize....

Part of a fucking poem.

Used to be one of Kat's favourites....

I get me that shudder...

"From here to there...

The Out Inside...

To crack the Sky....

The GREAT DIVIDE...."

One of Jeremiah King's...

The country's most famous poet...

Before he went batshit fucking crazy and became...

Became what?

A psycho?

A lunatic?

A fucking super villain?

Before he became...

THE BAD POET?

A noise distracts me...

I make with the sudden turn...

Bolt gun in my sweaty, twitchy hand...

No fucker there. Just Val....

Hanging...

Again....

Like a blocked fucking drain...

Soft.

Fluid.

Regular...

I take some steps...

Mr fucking cautious....

And then...

I fucking know where it's coming from...

I have to look....

Wish I hadn't....

Her stomach is moving....

Pulsing....

Get me some sickness...

Ignore it.

He didn't have time....

No careful insertion.

Just a gaping hole and the shard of mirror....

Stuffed

Mirror painted black as usual...

An eye scratched in the paint...

But behind it?

A bag?

A Pod?

Moving to some fucked up dance.....

Throbbing....

Pulsing.

I tell myself not to...

Ignore my fucking self and lean forward...

Grab the edge...

Pull the fucking mirror out.

SWEET

FUCKING

LORD.......

That's no bag...

No Pod.

It's a fucking nest.

Spun with Silicon threads...

Delicate.

Deadly...

And I just fucking broke it....

Do me some recoil and watch the little fuckers tumble out...

Crawling over the fur...
The torso.

Falling onto the desk...sticking in blood

SYLPH SPIDERS....

Each one the size of a 50 Credit piece...

Bleached white.

Swollen.

Dripping ugly abdomen...

Angry all to fuck...

There's one on my sleeve...

My fucking sleeve!

I make with the flinging.

Watch it bounce off the wall...

Watch it scuttle away...

This guy may be insane but he's got himself some fucking balls..

This size they can knock you out for hours.

Fuck you bad.

But the adults?

But the adults...

The adults are the size of real old style cats...

Remember those?

Put you in a fucking coma...

The long kind...

Feel the wall at my back...

Do the slow shuffle.

Play it cool Kurt..

Cool.

Punch my WristCom...

Get Gordon.

Call it in....

I order:

A DeFest Squad...

Lock down this whole fucking floor...

Call an evacuation.

Make some swearing.

Some BAD swearing.

Nasty surprise you fuck...

But another slip...

These bastards only live in one place...

Home.

The sewers beneath the fucking Pyramid.

That's where they originated...

New species.

Born out of the filth and shit that stinking place pumps out...

Mutated little fucks...

And no one...

I mean NO ONE, gets near to the Pyramid without a Pass Card...

Fucking invisible or not.

I'm getting closer to you. Bastard

Edge myself around the walls...

Nearly at the doors now...

Can't help but wonder how he got the nest away from the mother?

These fuckers are territorial...

Permanently pissed off.

Angry.

Aggressive.

If they ever migrate we are royally fucked...

Things are starting to come together...

Old gears beginning to grind...

I will find you, you bastard...

Know this.

For sure...

Deep breath...

I've reached the doors...

Push them...

Wait for them to slide.

Eyes trained on those nasty scuttling little fuckers...

And then...

Then that's when I feel it....

Something heavy landing on my shoulder...

Do a stagger.

Welcome some fangs...

Right side of my neck.

BURNING....

Figure I just found out where mummy fucking went....

Dizziness washes me down...

Nausea...

THE

WORLD

TURNS

BLACK.................

They say you experience nothing in a coma...

Just darkness and a loss of time...

You ask me?

People say all kinds of stupid shit...

Sunlight...

Fucking sunlight and that old forgotten warmth...

Feel my bones singing...

I know this place...

I know.

I fucking remember...

Primrose Hill?

Glorious green bathed in dancing light....

I'm down by the Shaman Sheath....

Fucking ice cream in my hands.

Younger hands

Sonic Hawks are doing their shit...

I figure it's the Noon Show...

I can see their handlers dressed in Chromium Safe Suits...

A hand in mine...

Sudden wave of long cherished scent.

Deep floral musk of sex...

Soft lips at the back of my neck...

Tickles...

"Cheer up Mr Grumpy....smile for me?"

Kat?

Fuck me...

Hello sweet kitten...

I'm sorry but I'd forgotten just how beautiful you were...

"C'mon Mr Wolf....let's go watch the show."

Her hand in mine....

A mingle of fur...

Drop the fucking ice cream...

Feel a smile...

"Sure thing kitten, let's go...."

I'm pulling her up the hill...
But she's staying still...

Quizzical face going on...

"Kurt?"

"Kurt! Don't forget the baby..."

The fuck?

There's a CarryPod at my feet...

An Electro Blanket...

Hands.

Tiny pink fingers...

A child?

Kat's bending down...

Pulling something small and perfect from the Pod...

Got me a sadness going on...

Unbearable...

We don't have a kid?

"I'll take her Kurt...you carry the Pod..."

The kid's beautiful...

Soft down...

Red shining hair...

Strange glowing eyes...

I'm crying...

"Sshhh little one...I know, I know...grumpy old daddy forgot you..."

Kid giggles...

So does Kat...

"Daddy's an old silly isn't he, Amelia"

Like a punch in the fucking gut...

That name...

AMELIA?

The scene flickers and goes...

Static...

Figure I make with a scream...

A ticket booth...

Old style...

When the underground was full of Shuttle Trains and not only Vermin Splices and mutants...

Booth 23?

Attendant's a Mouse Splice...

Filthy uniform...

Eyes stitched shut with copper wire.

Caked dried blood...

This doesn't seem to faze me.

"Payment?" He says...

Not sure how...his fucking mouth is sewn shut too...

Pat my pockets for credits...

Fucker shakes his head.....

"No Detective....Real Payment..."

Before I know it the bastard's stuck a scalpel in my paw...

Blood makes with the splatter...

He laughs.

Don't seem to feel it...

The Booth has gone...

Just me and a ticket...

Turn it over.

'THE LODGE...ONE WAY ONLY'

I hear beeping.

A Bell?

Mirrors...

Every fucking wall...

Like some kinda old school fucking carnival...

But get this...

No reflections...

In every one...a mouth.

Stretched...

Distorted...

Too long.

Too wide...

Upside down.

And they're laughing

Fucking laughing...

The noise is deafening....

Some guy...

in the corner...

Doing the weeping....

He sees me.

Fear in his eyes...

Shaking.

I know you...

I know you, you fucker.....

Joshua fucking Knight....

He's got something in his hands...

Something glowing...

He says:

"Wake me up?

Please, please wake me up?!"

Everything slides...

A jumble of fucking images and sound...

A room. Beads, incense, Noonian Spheres....

A figure in a chair.

An Owl?

Fuck but she's old...

Older than me...

Older than fucking time...

Grey feather shit going on...

She smiles at me...

Indicates a chair...

"13 months to this very day....

On the day of Wind and Fire you will come to me young Wolf....

You will come to me with questions."

"You will ask me for directions and I shall tell you

NORTH...

The Key will be with you...

She must be protected...

She will be afraid..."

"This is only a skirmish Detective....

Foreplay, if you will...

All will become clear on the day the Rain shall dance with the Fire...."

I feel something...

Out there in the Real...

A kiss?

Musk of a cat but not Katrina...

A voice.

"Wake up you old bastard."

Ren?
Owl grabs my hand...

Fading now.

Says:

"Two things young Wolf....

'An eye for an eye'

And

'Ladybird, ladybird... Fly away home....'"

Nothing...

Just a shroud of fucking grey static....

I can hear regular beeping...

A chlorine fucking stench...

Hint of light....

A final vision?

A cell?

Young boy in a Red Leather Combat Bodysuit...

Holding a balloon...

An orange balloon...

Turns...

Pluto?!?

"Save my brother, Mr Lobo?

Save us all?"

He hands me the balloon...

And yet...

And yet...

it's not a balloon...

It's the fucking Sun....

BLACKNESS....

SOUNDS...

"He's responding....

I think he's coming out of it...."

I drift again....

Beeping.

Beep

Beep

Beeping....

My eyes are open...

Are my eyes open?

I can taste Wolf...
The room stinks of it...

A figure in a chair....

DAD????

The fuck?

Dad's been dead for years you stupid old fuck...

I see the figure rise....

Approach...

Tubes up my fucking nose.

Wires...

"Heads up Bro....you been gone a long fucking time....."

It's Lyca...

It's my brother...

Lyca...

Feel a sob slip away....

Throat makes some noise...

Sounds like 'How long?'

He grabs my paw...

REAL....

"Two months Boss..."

What the fuck?

I'm back...

Back...

Much of the next few hours consists of drifting...

One minute I'm here...

The next, it's blackness...
I can smell my brother.
Clean sheets

I open my eyes and some Blackbird is making with the noise...

Holding a MediScan to my head...

Fuck, but my throat is dry...

I'm being given a lecture...

Stern faced fucker...

I decide not to give one back.

Not right now.

Feel so damn weak...

Like a pup...

"One more bite Detective and not even our wonder drug will save you."

He gives it that big pause...

I let him.

Dramatic little fuck...

"And another thing. It is rare for a patient to exit a coma healthier than when they entered it...."

Gives me the eye.

The medical one...

"I would suggest you modify your, er, lifestyle choices..."

I give him a laugh...

Sounds like broken glass.

Make with a beckon....

"Tell me Doc....is ReGen still legal?"

Puzzled face.

"Why of course it is..."

"Then there's your fucking answer..."

He doesn't say bye...

I can hear Lyca making with the laughter...

Turn my head...

Room does some whack ass dancing...

Make some noise.

"Gimme brother...."

"Kurt?"

"I can fucking smell it bro...pass it over...."

He becomes smiles...

Passes me a clear bottle...

My hands do a fumble thing...

Open....

At last!

Take a heroic fucking swig...

Make some less heroic coughing...

Like a fucking teenage pup...

Watery eyes....

Second hit...

Smoother now.

Fuck me but that's good...

Ride the dirty burn for a while...

Attempt me some of that speaking....

"News?"

He props himself on my bed....

All impeccable black suit and white tie.

"Nothing....

He's been quiet.....waiting...."

"Yeah....

Waiting for me...

The fucker seems to think I'm important..."

"You are bro...to some of us."

Feel a smile....

Swallow it...

"The kid?"

"He's fine Kurt...been here every day...even Mary popped by.

So did Agent Zelen..."

I nod.

"I know...I felt her...."

He wants to ask.....

But he lets it go.

He's a good brother.

Understands me...

We understand each other...

"She said to either hug you or punch you when you got back..."

Laughter.

More broken glass...

"I'll settle for the fucking punch..."

The door does that opening shit...

Some young nurse...a deer splice?

Breakfast is here....

I say some bad things....

Breakfast goes away

I sit up....

Am I sitting up?

Fuck yeah I'm sitting up...

Feel that head fandango....

Cough.

"Clothes......"

Lyca makes a face....

I ignore it...

"Clothes, brother. Now!"

He's got some guilt going on....

"Tell me Lyca?!"

"Kurt....

I wasn't here man....they...
Well, they cleaned them..."

I'm lost...

"So?
Seems pretty regular to me kid...what's the problem?"

He makes with the pale...

"Kurt....they cleaned them all....

Even your coat..."

MY COAT????

"MY FUCKING COAT?!"

He looks away...

"And....

And your hat Bro....."

Fuck me...

Can this day get any worse?

Welcome fucking back old man...

I choose to ignore these facts.

Takes me 30 minutes to get dressed....

30 fucking minutes...

The Vodkacaine helps...

So do the Stimms Lyca breaks under my nose....

Do me a stagger....

My back isn't complaining for the first time in decades...

Legs compensate by giving me that jelly vibe...

Traitors...

Locate the mirror...

Oh sweet fuck...

I look like an advert for smart living....

Clean.

Ironed.

Bright fucking eyed...

Shit.

Some fucker gave me a Sonic Shower while I was out....
I'm all brushed smart fur...

Still greying, you bastards...

Still greying....

I swallow any curses with a slug of juice....

Strap the holster.

Stroke the gun...

Attach my WristCom....

Turn to my brother.

Say...

"Let's get the fuck out of here...

Buzz the kid....

I need a fucking ride...."

Lyca grabs my arm.

I try not to fall over....

Hands me a folded paper...

A letter.

"A friend left this for you...

An old friend."

Real paper....

Real fucking ink...

I know who it's from...

ROACH.....

A letter from a dead man....

'Dear Kurt........'

Roach Monroe...

The city's finest, dirtiest journalist...

Dead now for over two years...

Don't ask.

It's kinda confusing....

'Welcome back you old bastard...we both know you're too gnarly to die....

Watch yourself old friend...

This is dark.

Dangerous.'

'They went looking for things that don't want to be found...

Actually, that's a lie...

They went looking for things that long to be found'

'Trust no one Kurt....

You need to look where your eyes can't and don't want to see....

Oh....and one last thing old man....'

'When Emily tells you her true name you must trust her totally...

You MUST listen.

Listen to her...

All the best.

Monroe.'

I think I grunt...

Put it in my pocket...

I'm not back enough for this kinda weird shit...

Do a stagger...

Push the door...

The corridor's too fucking bright.

A couple of nurses do that concerned bustle thing...

Lyca growls...

They go away.

Nice one bro...

In the lift I ignore my neon reflection...

I don't recognize that Wolf...
Check the messages on my WristCom....

Junk feeds.

The kid.

Ren.

Officer Cooper...
And one from Sanderson....

'Detective....we NEED to talk!!!'

I ignore it...

File it for later.

Why Kurt?

Why are you so fucking dumb?

Regret starts here....

It's with me to this day....

Floor 32....a Nurse gets in holding a head in a canister...

Looks like a Droid Splice...

Creepy fucker is looking straight at me....

Slowly it slides its eyes to gaze at the far corner of the lift...

No one there...

Then back to me...

Over and over again...

Find myself captivated...zone out of the conversation....

Stomach does a turn as the head opens its mouth.

An 'O'

Like a fucked goldfish

Floor 5....

The lift doors open and close....

No one gets in or out...

I don't give it a thought...

Fucks sake Kurt!!!

Like I said....

SLOPPY....

You stupid old man....

Fucking sloppy.

No goddam excuse...

We reach the foyer and I hear LYCA say something...

I've not heard a single word so I opt for

"Whatever..."

He gives me a strange look...

I cross the entrance hall as quick as my body lets me...
Trust me...it ain't quick...

Get a dizzy thing.

Ignore that fucker...

The Dust greets me.

The Dust and the swollen Moon.

Street seems too loud.

Too fucking real.
Lyca steadies me...

An arm.

There she is....

My Car...

And don't you know it?

It's been cleaned.

Swallow bad words.

Feel Lyca grinning at me...

Fucker.

The Kid's outta the car before I can snarl at my brother...

He's all smiles and nervous energy...

Kinda touched.

Don't let it show...

He bounds up the steps and for one horrible fucking moment I think he's gonna hug me.

The fucker does....

I let him.

Feels OK.

"Boss!!!

Boss....you're looking good!!"

Swallow me some bile.

Some sarcasm....

"Hey Kid....

You been OK?

What did I miss?"

"The usual Boss...the city's been pretty quiet...."

He's looking deep into my face.

Not sure what he expects to find...

Not sure myself...

I make with the back slapping...

Turn away.

"C'mon kid....

It's time we made some tracks...."
Glance at my brother...

Eye contact.

"Cheers Bro....
Guess it's time you got back to making some credits...."

He smiles....
"I'm always making credits brother...."

Walks away.

So do I.

We don't look back.

Say nothing.

No need...

It's what brothers do...

The car stinks of polish and pine...

Strong.

Heavy.

I almost puke...

Crack me a window.

Breathe some dust and fumes...

"Where to Boss?"

I give him the look.

The Lobo look.

A little rusty but it still seems to work.

"Where do you think kid?"

He gives me a sigh...

But that's OK...

I'm used to them.

"Sure...of course....OK."

Turns the key...

And we're systems go...

Music kicks in as we pull away and the Kid makes to kill it...

I do that hand thing....

"Leave it Kid...."

"Leave it on...."

Recognize it...

Kid's got taste.

The PHAZELORDS last album....

SHARDSONGS.

I sing along....

Fuck with his head.

Savour a secret.

"Me and Johnny go way back..." I say.

He gives me a glance.

Figures I'm fucking with him...

Maybe I am....

"How long we been partners Kid?"

He doesn't pause....

"3 and a half years Boss."

I nod and reach into my inside pocket....

Find what I'm looking for....

Battered and real....

Paperback.

THE SEARCH FOR JOHNNY PHAZE.

Pass it over.

Figure it's time...

"Read this Kid....

Geldof....

There's stuff you don't know about me....

I may be ancient but I sure ain't fucking dead..."

The rest of the journey is silent....

Save for the music....

The pounding

Soaring

Music....

Follow me some memories....

We reach the FORGETTING ROOMS.....

Kid kills the engine....

Goes to say something....

Thinks better of it....

Pulls a face.

Ease myself out of the car...only swear once...

Hear him turn the keys...

Reach out.

Grab them.

"Not this time Kid...today you come in."

His face is priceless...

I enjoy it for a while.

Lock the door...

Pocket the keys.

"C'mon Kid....the drink's not gonna drink itself..."

Nod to the Rhino on the door...

Go inside...

Droids not working....just some girl.

Says her name's Sally....

Grab us some seats...

Kid's flustered.

Sweating?

"3 beers sweetheart....3 chasers......"

She builds the drinks...all lips and hips....

I shake my head....

"No Babe.....no....

You misunderstood.....

I meant 3 each...."

Geldof does that pale thing....

I stifle a laugh...

I slide them over....

"But, Boss....Mary doesn't like me drinking...."

I make with a gesture....

"You see Mary here Kid?"

The first one slides down like forgotten liquid heaven....

Out of the corner of my eye I see the kid take a gulp...

A good damn gulp...

"Thing is Kid...she'll be pissed with you...sure...

Shout maybe...

And then forgive.

That's what lovers do...

What partners do..."

"Tell me Kid....

You ever counted her fucking shoes?"

He snorts beer from his lame ass snout....

Sets me off laughing....

Feels good.

Neck the rest....

Slam the first shot.

Kid does the same....

Glowing.

Feel that dirty welcoming buzz....

"Lyca tells me you were there every day Kid....

Every day...."

I let it hang....

He ignores my eyes...

Men, eh?

Stupid fucking men...

Next time I look he's halfway through the next brew...

Quick learner.

"I appreciate it Kid....

Partner...."

I leave it at that.

Enough.

By the time we order the next 3 I've told him about Vapour Park...

He's told me about his mother...

Man stuff.

Friend stuff....

I nearly mention Katrina.....

It's all going swell till the WristCom beeps and delivers the news....

That dirty fucking news.....

It takes us ten minutes to reach the crime scene.

On foot.

The kid's kinda glassy eyed and there's no fucking way I should be behind a wheel.

The Night's doing that dusty thing...

A sense of drizzle in the air.

We don't talk much.

Shit...we don't talk at all.

As we cross the intersection at Smith and Baker he shoots me a look.

"Boss...It sounded kind of bad."

I make with a growl.

"They always sound bad, Kid...

And you know what?

They usually fucking are..."

I can see the building now...

All glass and carved stone.
There's a small crowd gathering.

I wave Mr BoltGun and they take the fucking hint...

Melting away like ThermoCubes in neat Vodkacaine...
The kid's looking upwards...turns a shiter shade of pale.

"Boss?"

I don't wanna look up...fuck me, I don't even wanna be here...

Something wet and red lands on my coat.

I make with the bravery, swallow something bile coated and tilt
my head.

Fuck me...

The Chapel of The Visiting Lord...

That giant stone head gazes down on me...

All slanted almond eyes and Ebony chiselled hair...

And...

And hanging from the neck...on industrial wires, like some sick
kinda necklace...

A girl.

Dripping.

If I reached up a hand I could touch her feet...

Fuck that...keep my hands where they are.

Take a deep breath.
Watch her gently swing.

The blood's dripping from between her legs...

LycoJeans stained deep dark red.

Smells young...no older than sixteen.

Some kinda generic Mammal Splice...
all soft fur and whiskers.

Look higher...

There's the steel spike...behind the ear, slightly obscured by the addition of a bright red wig.

Squint a little. Trust my eyes.
Silver glints in neon light.

Nails.

The bastard nailed the wig on her.

And the eyes...

There's something not right about the eyes.

Fish in a pocket. Locate my torch. Flip it on.

Reflections.

Purple reflections...

Glass? Plastic?

Purple glass forced into the eye sockets...

Feeling kinda cold.

Tasting something bad.

The kids taking VidShots...crazy white flashes illuminate the scene.

I sigh...

Jesus I sound fucking old.

Turn my attention to the placard hung around her neck...

Words daubed in thick black ink.

'WELCOME HOME DADDY.'

Turn away...make with a retch.

The Fucker knows!

Been in my fucking head...

How the fuck can he do that?

"Boss?"

The kid's giving me that look.

"Is this some sort of clue? A message for someone?"

Hear myself snarl...

"Yeah, Kid, It's a message...For me."

Pause old man...breathe.

"I'm gonna get this bastard Geldof...

Make the fucker pay."

He's lost...can see him fight the urge to ask questions.
Good kid. He's learning.

Sirens in the distance...figure the Meat Wagons on its way.
Turn away. Drag on my cigar.

Make a decision.

Nothing more here for me...too damn soon.

Old head not firing on all cylinders yet.

I've seen what the bastard wanted me to see.

"Kid? Take it from here, ok?

I need a walk...clear my fucking head....

I'll leave my comm open..."

"Sure thing Boss...you need to rest up.

Maybe eat something?"

He's all concern and fidgets...swallow the urge to slap him.

"Yeah...food. I'm on it. And Kid?"

"Kurt?"

"Anything new...anything at all and you call me. Get me?"

"Sure Boss...go rest."

Turn and walk away...don't look back old man. Don't look back.

There's a beeping from my WristCom and I give it a look.

The Witch again. Not now Witch.
Hit a button and send it straight to file.

Some things are there to haunt us...

Stupid Wolf.

Figure I'll take the East walk home.

There's thirteen bars on this route...

I know them all and they sure as hell know me.

By bar three I'm feeling much more back in the zone.

Got that fume mouth going on.

At the corner of Guardian and Cooper the Zebra Girls all wave and suggest things long forgotten.

I give them a smile and move on.

Some street Rats give me the eye...think better of it.

Smart Rats.

So...

This guy's invisible...

No scent...

Knows me and can read minds...

But a fucking coma?
Never heard of a Psych who can travel that deep...

Fuck...never heard of an invisible man either.

This damn city's full of fucking surprises.

Not sure just when it happens but I begin to notice something...on the edges.

Playing hide and seek with the Vodkacaine....what is it?

A scent?

Hell yeah...

It's that burning electrical smell again....

Faint but growing stronger.

Turn off my mind and let the snout do its thing...

GOT IT!

Cross the street...

Give the finger of the law to an overzealous driver...

Slow the fuck down moonshine.

Walk me some streets...then some sidestreets.

Stronger now...

Dancing light above the stench of rubbish bins and fucking despair.

Gotcha...

A doorway in the side of the old PrintWorks.

The door's open.

'Course it is...

Door's been forced.

Lock cut clean...thermo lance.

Figure nobody's been in here for years...

Figure the stench of damp and decay might make me spew...

Figure I should just swallow and man the fuck up.

BoltGun's in my paw...finger resting easy.

There's a faint glow in here...

A Luminance Globe sits pulsing on an abandoned worktop.

Everything shrouded in mildew and dust.

Move closer...Two objects.

Clean.

New.

A bottle...

Old style stopper...real fucking cork...
And a handwritten note.

'SMELL ME.'

Next to it...
A sheet of laminated paper...
And another note.

'READ ME.'

Figure what the hell...move closer...

The paper first...eyes are growing used to the light...

'What is Science but MAGIKS by another name?...
He WAITS for you Detective.

He WAITS in the BONE TEMPLE.'

Make with a soft growl...I hate this mystical shit.

Shuffle over to the bottle.
Weigh me some options.

Poison?

Nerve Agent?

Who fucking cares?

Pop the cork...wince...

Still breathing.

Here goes nothing.

Raise it to my snout.

There it is!

That electric trail.
Heavier...like a brand new appliance...

Like burning dust.

Like the scent of a killer?

Replace the bottle and take in the rest of the room.

Too damn dark in the corners.

Flick my torch...pupils dancing in the sudden glare.

The fuck is that?

In the far corner.

A chair?

Again, it's new...

All metal and tubes...

Parts of it look fashioned from cold white bone...

Armrests carved into clenched claws....

And another note.

'SIT IN ME.'

I actually laugh...

"Don't think so Moonshine...
I'm dumb but I sure as hell ain't that dumb..."

Smell the Phermonica seconds before I feel the needle enter my neck...too damn slow Kurt!

As darkness wraps I hear a soft, musical voice.

"Oh but I insist Detective...

I really do insist..."

BACK!

Only seconds I guess...maybe a minute.

Body's out for the count but everything above my neck seems to be working...

Give my eyes a second to reboot and focus.

I'm sitting in the damn chair.

There's a figure before me.

Black hooded robe and a mask.

A glittering silver mask.

A Crow's head...blue jewels for eyes.

I know this man.

It's the Poet...

The BAD POET.

Shit.

Make with a cough...

"If you're gonna do it Poet at least make it fucking quick..."

The mask inclines like he's listening to far away voices.

Figure he may be.

"Now now now Detective...you know I cull only the unworthy and impure.

No my old friend, I bring not the blade but assistance...

As I did once before."

And back comes the memory...that hidden fucking moment.

My apartment. So long ago.
I've still got her blood on my fucking clothes.
No more tears.
All cried out.
A knock on the door.
Open it like I'm sleepwalking.
Same figure.
Same robes.
Different mask.
A bronze Bears head.
"I have a present for you Lobo...a reward, if you will."

He's watching me.

"You must miss her very much...even now, after so many many years?"

Don't answer...

I couldn't even if I wanted to.

"Tell me Lobo, do you ever revisit that room?

The chamber?"

Try to laugh...

Sounds more like a scream.

"Every fucking night Poet when I close my fucking eyes."

"I meant in person. I do.
Once a month.
The field still functions.
He's still there.

Sometimes I even take salt..."

More image flashes.
Wires. Chains.

Peeled skin...

Fuck me Kurt...

Push it away! Forget.

"But now is not the time for recollections, is it?

Now is the time for words

And the seeding of actions."

He moves towards me.

Moves like his weird ass voice.

Musical.

All fluid and odd angles.

All wrong.

"Do you like your seat Detective?
I made it for you.

The dimensions were rather hard to locate but I persevered.
It is said to bring wisdom.

Dark, unsettling wisdom.

Is it working Lobo?
Is the Forbidden Throne of Set speaking to you?
Will you hear his knowledge?

His call through the ages?"

"You need help Poet...serious fucking help."

"Possibly...

But for now I am the Agent of help...

I bring directions for the one you seek.

The Meddler in things he does not understand, yet covets so very,
Very
Much."

Try to move.

Not a thing.

"Go on?"

"He seeks the Divide, Lobo.

He would summon the GREAT DIVIDE.

Yet not for the cause of Lady Balance.

No, he believes it will bring him power.

The power of the Forgotten Lonely Gods.

He meddles, Detective.
He meddles in my affairs.
The fluctuations grow harder to manipulate.

To control."

Manage a laugh. A real one this time. Give it that old Kurt lip curl.

"You know so much about him?
He's messing up your wacky little sandpit?
Then why the fuck haven't you taken him out yourself?"

A pause.

Swear he's scowling beneath that silver mask.

"You think I have not tried?

I have sent countless of my Golems to find him...

All to no avail.

The Shroud keeps him hidden and secure. And"
He taps the side of his mask.

"The Passenger makes him smart.

No Detective I cannot locate that which is so hidden but you...
He wants you to find him.
He waits for you.
Taunts you.
Fears what you may or may not be in this skewed Celestial Dance...

You Lobo are the one to find him.

Stop him."

We let the silence in. Consider some stuff. I break first.

"What you got?"

"You have all you need, you just have to let it form...

The Throne will aid you with this.

What else to say?

He owns, or has seen, parts of The NUMERICON but he misunderstands.
He craves that which was never intended nor foreseen.
He is dangerous Kurt. More so than even he knows.
We are at a crossroads in Universal Flux you and I.

Mummers in a play long written.

If you can't find him Detective he will break the all...find him.

You now have the directions.

The map."

Heads pounding. Swimming in and out.
Swear to fuck I'm seeing shit that ain't even there.

I make some kinda noise.

"Relax Kurt...The Throne is taking you.

Let it speak.

LISTEN!

But now, before I depart...we will meet again Detective.

Stand side by side even.

Something comes.

Something beyond your ken..."

"Yadda yadda...the Storm...blah fucking blah.

Seems every fucker wants to warn me about the fucking weather..."

Faint now...I'm slipping.

But I catch his final words.

"No Kurt...

I speak not of the Beast and the Storm,

That chapter will run its course.

I speak now of something new.
Something that comes from the very edges of the Now.
Something mournful, angry and alone...

I speak of The SHADOW.

I have seen her in the MEDUSA SHARD...

Darkness will fall upon us all....

Now shhh.....sleep Detective....

Let the visions of wisdom come...."

And that's all she wrote....

Wake up hours later in the sidestreet opposite my apartment.
Clean clothes all fucked up with mud and grime...
Figure he got one of his Golems to carry me home.

The thought gives me the shudders.

Consider calling the kid...sending a squad.
What's the point?
The room will be empty and clean.
That's what the Poet does...

He melts away.

Move my head...

Feeling good. No swimming.
No slidy fucking crap.
Body feels warm.

Relaxed even.

Then it hits me.

I know.

I fucking know.

MAGIKS?

The BONE TEMPLE?

Fuck me old man...how long have you fucking lived here?

Get me the urge to go running off.

Deal with this shit right now but part of me tells me to sleep. Plan. Go in there fresh...

Truth be told it kinda sounds like Kat's voice.

Take me a moment. Relent.

The aches are coming back...

Better to go in prepared.

Get to my feet and shuffle across the street.
Not sure of the time but the streets are empty...
An Ad Bot blinks feebly in my direction...
He's out of luck.

Guess I'm too old for Breast Augmentation.

Foyer's dark.

Take the stairs...me and the lift have history. Bad history.

Turn the corner. Feel the neck prickles.

My door.

Open.

Wide fucking open.

Heads up Kurt...

Think about reaching for my gun.
Think again...
Whoever's in there is gonna be sliced and diced to fuckery.
Guess I'm gonna need a CleanSquad not a fuckin gun.

Cautiously enter.
It's the smell that hits me first...something hot and deep.

Food?

Fucking food?

The side light's on.
If my pit could ever be called cosy then now's the time.
Confusion does its thing. And then...

There she is.

Cross legged on the rug.
Battered leather and weird ass shades.

The girl from down the hall.

EMILY?

She's smiling...

"How the fuck did you get in here kid?"

A giggle...like a song.

"I used the door Mister Wolf...It's what they're for..."

"No...you know what I mean...
This place is DaisyChained...

You should be mincemeat..."

"Oh...The Naughty Number String Detective?

I sang them to sleep...even numbers like songs don't you know?"

I'm feeling kinda lost.
Should be angry but I'm feeling strange.

Calm?
Fuck me it's been a long time.

She's on her feet.

Pulling me towards the couch.

Helping me out of my coat.

There's a sheet thrown over the MirrorCam.
A clean sheet.
Fuck only knows where she found that. I gesture.

"The fuck is this?"

That giggle again. Nectar notes.

"I'm hiding from my Father Sweet Wolf. It wouldn't be wise to be found just yet..."

Time's getting fractured.

Next thing I know there's a bowl in my hands.

Despite myself I feel my old mouth salivate.

"Eat sweet one...you need to be strong to complete the puzzle."

"What fucking puzzle?"

"The Bone Puzzle mister Wolf...
And I am the final piece...

Now shush and eat."

I don't know what this is but it sure ain't Gar meat.
I give her the questioning look.

"My sister and I know where the Wild Things grow Kurt...relax
and enjoy it."

Time again. Gone. Bowl clean. Fuzzy.

Suddenly notice that Katrina's HoloFrame has been turned to
face the wall.

Make to get to my feet but she's in my lap.

Holding my face...

Soft.

"She wouldn't want to see this Kurt...trust me."

Then there's a tongue.

Long.
Sweet.
Probing.

Jasmine and Cinnamon and Daylight.

The rest is mine. Mine and mine alone.

SLEEP.

Open my eyes.

First damn morning in an age I haven't coughed myself awake.

Eyes adjust slowly and she's there.
By the door.
Fully clothed.
Got that calm shit going on.

Her shades are on the bedside table.

I make with the call.

"Emily? Your glasses..."

She turns. Hand leaving the door handle. Pads quietly back to the bed. Her eyes, beneath the thick red hair are glowing.

Purple.

"They are your shades now sweet Wolf...you will need them..."

And she bends, cupping my ear.

Whispering.

"And today Kurt my name is not Emily. Today I am....."

The name is lost in a fuzz of cold delight....
But I hear it.

I hear it.

I'm alone.

Takes me an hour to get dressed.

An hour to function.

Strap on my gun.

Give the room a glance.

Remove the Mirror sheet.
Think about it.
Leave the HoloFrame as it is.

The girl was right.

She wouldn't want to see this.

Especially what must come next.

Close the door. Go to meet my brother.

Lyca's waiting for me at Ennis and Burroughs.

Black suit.
Black shirt.
White tie.
Black leather
And, get this,

White fucking socks.

He see's my expression and smiles.

"One of us had to be born with style Bro."

I shake my head and gaze up at the Pyramid, looming over us.
Cold. Unsettling.

"Magiks...." I mutter to myself.

Lyca's sniffing the air. Fucker's grinning.

"Kurt...oh Kurt!

Tell me Bro, who was the lucky girl?"

Sees my face.

Shuts the fuck up.

I make with the questions.

"You sure this is gonna work?"

Suddenly he's all business.

Waves a KeyCard under my nose.

"No problem Kurt.
One of the benefits of dancing with the Devil is that it opens
certain doors...

Follow me."

We cut across the street.
Down Bowie Plaza and out into the loading bay.
Area's bathed in Cuckoo beams.
He flashes the Card.
Opens his eyes wide.
Cuts a beam.

No alarms go off.

"The doors over there."

He's pointing at a blank stone wall.

I give him the shrug and he steps forward.

Slides the Card into the tiniest of fucking cracks and

Hey Fucking Presto.

A door.

Grins like a loon.

"Shall we?"

We go inside.

I hate this place.
It's the smell.
Equal parts hospital and tomb.

The sounds don't help either.
Drills. Moaning. Screams.

The boy points me towards a lift.

"Welcome to the Chocolate Factory Bro..."

An in-joke. A shared childhood joy.

There's bloodstains on the lifts floor.
I make with the ignore.
Stark white light bathes us.

Floor 32.

We get out.

The Trooper in Riot Gear kinda wishes we hadn't.

She brings her gun to bear.

Lyca's quick...quicker than me...
Grabs the barrel, delivers a kick.
The girl's good.

Too fucking good.

Twists. Turns. Brings the butt down on the Boy's snout.

Crimson sprays my jacket.

The crazy fucker's laughing as he takes her feet from beneath her. Right arm twisted behind her back.
Gun kicked away.

"Hold your horses Trooper and take a look at this...
Check who authorized it..."

He's pushing the card in her face.
Snout dripping shit on her suit.

She relaxes and he lets her go.
Warily get to their feet. Do some talking.

Me? I'm kinda zoned out. Still got that calm going on....

Seems their chinwag's over.

She retrieves her weapon and Lyca leads me away.

"Cool Kid...nearly had me." Wipes his fucked up nose.
I give him the brotherly look...

"You gave her your number didn't you?"

He laughs. Lyca laughs a lot.

"Life's short Bro...you know that..."

We do some walking. Ignore the noises.

Whole fucking place seems deserted.

"The Snake likes his privacy," explains Lyca, stopping outside a steel plated door.

I go to knock but he shakes his head.
Sprays me with blood.
Raises a foot and kicks the door open.
Gotta love him.

"Hello honey! We're home."

Follow him inside. Rooms all sickly yellow lighting and flashing terminals.

And there he is.

Behind the desk.
Grey suit and just a hint of scales.
The Devil's right hand man.

Sylvain.

Christ but I hate this fucker.

Gotta give it to him though...the fucker doesn't even flinch.

"Ahh...The Brothers Grim...how simply delightful.

Now, will you excuse me for a moment while I summon security?"

He's reaching for the Comm when Lyca plumps himself down on the desk.

"Not so fast Sparky...

Those Kallisti Cabal members you were after? Touch one fucking thing and I may just forget some names..."

Snake plays the game...

"But then you would surely lose out on quite a considerable amount of credits?"

The boy plays it better.
"Trust me Scales...I got credits...

Loads of credits."

Got him. He sits back and considers us.

Cold fucking eyes.

Nods.

"Very well...but first I think it wise that we...." Depresses a button in his right palm.
I go for my gun but Lyca shakes his head.

"Chill Kurt...It's just a dampening field."

Sylvain smiles...like how a corpse would smile.

"It's for the best Detective...The SCARECROW can get rather paranoid if he hears things not for his ears."

I remove my paw from my gun. He settles down and adopts some gracious.

"Now then Dogs...How can I assist you?"

We let the slur slide. Lyca gives me the floor. I take it.

"There's a killer out there Snake...a crazy fucking killer."

"The nature of the City I'm afraid Detective...

This concerns me because?"

"Cause he's fucking invisible and scentless..."

A flinch. A twitch.

"Invisible you say?"

"Yeah...you think of anyplace someone could make themselves that way? Anyplace you could find that kind of Tech?"

He raises a hand.

Kinda angry.

Kinda fearful?

I fucking hope so.

"Whatever you hear does not go beyond this room Lobo?

Your word. Give me your word."

I give it him. Begins with F.

He's punching buttons.
Images play on the monitors.

Diagrams.

Faces.

Figure I recognize one...A TigerSplice.
Yellow feather on a thong.

But the fecker's talking again.

"There was a theft. Eight months ago. One of our Projects was compromised."

I give him the go on gesture.

"Despite what you may believe Detective there are still frontiers to be explored.
Conquered.

We have been sending teams for quite some time.
None have returned.

We considered that maybe a more secretive method was required..."

Lycia's grinning...
Figure he already knows this...
Figure he knows plenty.

"Three suits were developed.
Three Void Suits with Stealth Technology...
Extremely expensive Stealth Technology...
One has been taken...

We would be more than grateful for its return."

Something stinks here...I wave at the terminals.

"Someone broke in and just took it?

Insider job I can get but this place...

This place is sewed tighter than a Witches ass...

You must have records? Vida records?"

"They were all unfortunately deleted."

"Bullshit...

It would take a fucking genius to pull this shit off...
You telling me there's a crazy fucking genius out there with Tech Grade weaponry?"

Lyca whistles soft.
Leans in close to the snake.

"He's got a WURM hasn't he?

You used the fucking WURM and now it's come back to bite your scaly ass..."

Sylvain giving him the glower.

I'm giving them both questions.

"The fuck is a WURM?"

Lyca turns towards me.

"A weapon Bro...
A weapon that doesn't kill...
It just modifies the victim.

Makes them think the things this place wants them to.

Wireless Urban Resistance Module...

Brainwashing a la carte...

But these fuckers can't ever deploy it...

There were problems weren't there Sparky?"

"What's up Snake? Your clever shit didn't work?"

I swear to god the fuck actually hisses at me.

"Oh it worked Hound. It worked too well.

The parasite became aware.

Outgrew its purpose...

The hosts attained an almost Messianic state of mind...we were forced to abort the tests.

To terminate them all."

"Not all of them it seems...and let me fucking guess...no records?"

"There was a fire...."

"Sure there was...Sure. So, last thing Snake...

How the fuck do I locate this bastard?"

The fucker laughs in my face.

"Oh but you don't Lobo...you don't.

That's the point of the suit."

I'm done here. Turn towards the door.
Consider shooting the fuck in the face.

Swallow it down.

The Boy follows me but the Snake grabs his arm.

"The names Lyca? The address?"

Lyca waves a claw...

"The moment we're one mile away from this place I'll send them you. Not a second before...

You get me Sparky?"

We leave the door open...

As we reach Morpheus Gardens Lyca's WristCom beeps.

One mile exactly.

He stops and lights a smoke.

Breaks the silence.

"Well that was fun wasn't it?"

I grab him by the arm.

"Bro...those names? The address...

You really gonna give him them?"

Tight smile.

"Of course I am Kurt...of course I am.

And you wanna know what the Shades will find?

A room.

Burnt out and vacated...such a shame.

The Cabal have agents everywhere....Guess someone alerted them."

I make with an apologetic grin. Keep talking.

"The other thing?

You got me the other things?"

He nods...fishes in his coat.
Hands me a small bag.

MicroMesh.

"Careful with this shit Bro...one nick and you're living a long painful life..."

Give him a grimace.

"Been there kid...done that."

He's twitchy. Got offers to make.

"You need me to get your back Bro?"

"Nah...no kid...this one's mine.

This bastard is mine."

Turn and walk away. Call over my shoulder.

"I'll be in touch."

He's already gone.

Takes me an hour to reach my destination.

Out by the Wall...

I should have known straight away.

The old Slaughter House from before the Fall.

The BONE TEMPLE...street slang.

Old and decayed now...

Demolition Notice fastened to the rusting gates.

"23.05" Five months time.

The gates are open. Chains broken. I expected no less.

The fucker's inside.

Waiting for me.

Ok Kurt...let's rock.

Let's fucking rock.

The hallway's full of junk. Ancient fucking junk.

Cans, rotting plastic bags...the odd white bone.

There's used condoms in here nearly as old as me.

Torch plays the floor.

Something's been here recently.

Fresh scuff marks cutting the tide of filth.

Something was dragged.

Something big.

Push me some big steel doors.

Enter a corridor of plastic sheeting and long ago stains.

Fuckers flap my face as I push through.

Onwards towards the Hall.
Smell hits me.

Strange.

Foul.

Flames and something rancid melting?

There's light spilling from the glass partitioned doors in front of me.

Flickering.

Kill my torch.

Take a moment.

Practice that deep, deep breathing.

Here goes nothing.

The Slaughter room's illuminated.

Gar wax candles placed everywhere.

On the circular stone walls of the Blood Pool (now dry as a fucking bone).
In every corner.
High above on both metal gantries.

Along the shaft of the great steel chimney.

Crazy fucking shadows going on.

But it's not the shadows that bring the chill.

The fear. The first sense of creeping dread.
The self hate.

No...It's what's hanging from the vast circular roof that hits me in my tired old guts like a Docker's dirty boots.
My old, stupid, lazy guts.

For fucks sake Kurt...what are you responsible for now?

Sanderson.

Fuck me Sanderson...forgive me.

She's hanging from high tensile shipping wires.

Tied to a wooden pole....

No, that's not a pole...
It's a Broomstick...
A fancy dress fucking Broomstick and she sure as hell ain't tied to anything.

I can see Staples. Builders Staples.

Heavy duty masonry staples.

She's raining blood like a sad fucking cloud...

The throat's been torn out...urgent and cruel. And the mouth...

Sewn shut with DroidWire...ugly purple bruises.

The eyes are gone.

On the far wall, daubed in red fluid (make a fucking guess) are the words SUFFER NOT A TRAITOR TO LIVE.

But there's a difference here.

This one was just for fun.

Just for me?

There's no silver rod behind the ear.
This was to make a fucking point.

Shit. I spoke to soon.

No rod?

I don't even see it coming. High speed. Fired from some kinda gun.

Just a silver streak and then burning fucking pain.

Hits me in the left thigh. Knocks me off my feet.

Jaw kisses the broken stone at the base of the Blood Pool.

Mind considers passing out.

Fuck that.

Say the bad word.

The really bad word.

The one my Dad taught me when the creeps at school began questioning our family's heritage.

Say it again.

SCREAM IT.

There's a chuckle.

Electronic and amplified.

The Bastard's wired up the whole building.

Distortion module kicked all the fucking way.

"Welcome to the Main Act Detective...I must say I expected you a little earlier...

You grow slow in your old age."

"Expect this you Fucking Freak!"

Pop above the crumbling wall. Spray some Bolts. Hear them impact metal and stone.

Laughter.

Crouch my ass down and grab the rod. Pull it quick and clean.

See myself some flashy white shit.

Vomit.

Scrabble in my pocket and crack a Stimm direct into the wound. Try not to scream.

Fucking fail.

Come on ReGen you bastard fucking shit...start that fucking knitting....

"Is that what they taught you at Law School old man?
Fire blind?

Into the dark?

The endless swirling dark?"

"They taught me that a sick cunt is a sick cunt, whether you can see the fucker or not."

Try four more shots. Duck from the rebounds.

"You know what I see when I look at you Wolf?
I don't see the Good Cop, the saviour.
The white fucking Knight on his valiant steed...

I see a waste.

An irritant.

A lonely old drunk who persists only on the goodwill of his peers.

I see blind hopeless ignorance."

"You coming on to me Freakshow?"

"And yet...since I found my new eyes I see more.

I see a Point in Flux.

A gateway.

You seem to stand in more than one world Wolf.

You seem to be important and Lobo...stupid, pathetic Lobo, I would eat that importance."

"Eat this!"

Chambers empty. Reload with shaking fucking paws.

"I am so full now, Wolf.

So full of dreams and fears and Souls...

I suspect that one more meal...one more important meal will open the Void and bring me that which is mine..."

If this fucker had anything left to lose then I figure he's just lost it. Shouting now.
Words I don't even recognize.

Gutteral sounds.

I make to peer and the wall above me erupts in masonry dust.

Semi Automatic I figure.

Military gear.

Figure I'm fucked.

Figure I can't see.

Wipe the grit from my streaming eyes. The air's just a drifting dusty minefield.

Dig in my pocket. Find the shades.

The Girl's Shades.

Put them on.

And that's when it all changes.

The room's like it's lit by PhosforStrips.

Feels like I got me some Droid Vision. Crystal.

Sharp.

Clear.

And there....on the second gantry.
A mess of colour.

Shifting and morphing.

Black, shot through with Red and Silver.

And now...

Now it's becoming recognizable.

A form.

A shape.

A man.

I take four shots.
Three hit clean.
Right shoulder.
Both kneecaps.

Fucker goes down like a sack of shit.

See a Riot Gun materialize and fall to the floor.

He doesn't make a fucking sound.

Takes me ten minutes to climb up there.

Legs knitting but screaming like a bitch.

I don't really notice it.

Standing before him now.

Shoot the other shoulder just for kicks.

Bend down. Grab the head...fiddle around until.

Got it.

Pop the clasp.

Remove the mask.

A head appears.

The Doberman.

Samuel.

White saliva coats his muzzle.

There's something in those eyes I never ever wanna see again.

"Too late Kurt...The Old Ones will come for me..."

"They better be fucking quick."

Blow his right ear off.

Gotta fucking sting.

He's panting.

"I have done enough to enter the Seventh Gate you stupid fucking Wolf...

I am beyond your fucking laws."

"Figure you're right about that."

And for a second it's years ago...standing before a door. Deep underground.

The Poet pushes it open.

"Vengeance Lobo.

Vengeance."

Takes me three punches to break the fuckers jaw. Looks like he's crying.

Fish in my pockets.

Two things first....

A bag. Empty it into my paw.

Twelve ReGen.

Grab his flapping jaw. Open wide Sunshine.

Force them in his mouth. Hold the muzzle closed.

The fucker swallows.

Next I get the roll of tape. DroidTape.

Industrial.

Wrap that fucking snout as tight as an unwanted Christmas present.

Leave the nose free.

Get kinda bored.

Blow the other ear away.

Now it's time for the icing.

Grab me the bag Lyca gave me.

Pull the cartridge from my gun and empty the bolts into my pocket.

Open the bag. Roll the contents out.

Five silver bolts.

Load them one by fucking one.

"You know what these are Samuel?
Course you do.

Course you do.

You're a fucking genius aren't you?

How's your passenger holding up by the way?

Kinda nervous I figure."

Staring right at me.

"But these are special Bolts.

Very very special.

Tell you the truth Freakshow they cost more than I earn a year but I figured, you and me?

Our relationship?

Hell, I figured you were worth it."

Watching me.

"Cause these babies...these babies are coated in something rare. Something Shadelike...you following?"

Narrow now. Understanding.

"These pretty little fuckers are covered in Anti-ReGen..."

At last I see it. The dread.
I fire twice to the stomach.

Three times in the groin.

Blow the barrel like an old style gunslinger.

Figure I'm a touch crazy right now.

Grab his head and replace the mask. Voila...the Lady Vanishes.

Drag him to the old chimney.

Got me some tape.

Got me some good solid steel.

Takes about Ten minutes.

Strapped good and tight.

Watch as the VoidSuit camouflages the tape....

Clever fucking Tech.

At the door I reload and locate the holding beams above Sanderson's body.

Do me some shooting.

Bring the roof down.

Rubble.

Nothing to see here kids.

I'll list her as M.I.A.

But I won't forget. I'll never fucking forget.

On the way out I check the Demolition Notice.

Five months...not long enough but I guess it'll do.

I don't look back.

There's no fucking need.

FIN.

EPILOGUE...

I watch the demolition from down by the old docks.

I like it here. No fucker comes here anymore.

Quiet.

Remember me a time we had real rats. All gone now.

Eaten.

Building goes up in seconds.

Figure I should feel something.

I don't.

I sense him before I hear him.

Hand on my gun.

"Kurt?"

Relax. Move my paw.

"Roach? You should be careful. You're dead remember?"

"Still am old friend. Still am. There's a thing. Something you need to see."

Passes me an InfoPad...Old school.

I don't look at him.

Too many damn Psychs these days.

Don't wanna know what he looks like.

Don't want anyone fishing.

"It's valid Kurt...my old number, before I died.

Only three people had it."

I thumb the screen. Words come into play...

"Hey Guys!

I think I've figured this SubWave Signal out at last.

Not sure just when or how it will reach you.

Just wanna let you Cats know I did it.

Made my way out of The BLACK WOODS.

I'm coming home Guys.

Coming home.

JOHNNY."

Detective Kurt Lobo will return soon...

PolyPhaze Productions thanks you for Gazing.

A BLACK BARD (Birth)

I was 6 years old when my toy bit me...
A Polymorphic class interactive Rabbit.
White.

The wound bled for a week.

I told no one....

Less than 12 months later I would perform the first of my Culls...
It involved a rock hammer...
A Turbo Bus...
And bleach.

Duncan his name.

Duncan was larger.
14.
A brute. He had begun to get inappropriate with my friend Sandra...
Violent.
I viewed his arousal with distaste...
I have no patience for Bullies.
For bad manners.
The Rock Hammer spawned a crimson Rose...
The Turbo Bus removed the clues...

The Bleach washed me....

CLEAN.

I recall the sweetest stinging...

That Christmas I confided in Sandra...
She was less than enthusiastic.

And so my second Cull occurred.

A pillow.

A screwdriver.

A mess.

I've been watching your apartment for 5 weeks now.
I know how your sheets smell.
How your clothes taste.

Your ROU
TI
NE

I have been adding my essence to your beauty products for 14 days.
My seed.

You face the world wearing me...
My beautiful new Angel.

My offering...

My love.

Maybe this time my formula will work...

My spell....

We can hope my love...

I am aware a storm is coming...
That soon I must leave this city...

I leave for you my journal.
My memories.

My confession...

My name?

I have had so many...as I have appearances....

My first name was Jeremiah Skald...

Jerry...
Sweet little Jerry...

You will know me by another brand...

The Poet.

The Bad Poet...

This is my song...

My crime.

I was a pale and uninteresting child.
Slender.
A waif.
This suited me fine...
I took to wearing glasses to heighten the effect.
Glass lens..

Words soon became my constant companion...
I grew to love the size, sound and beat...
The intangible flow.
The magic therein...
Secrets.

At the age of 9 I discovered numbers...
To be precise I discovered the work of Benjamin Glyph.
A once renowned numerologist....
Once...

By this time he had been denounced as a Heretic...
Dangerous.
I found the texts in the sealed library...
Dusty.
Forgotten.

Unique.

Glyph had spent his last years turning his mathematical eye to the Alphabet....

He claimed to have discovered the Prime Letter....

A key.

An undiscovered letter that unlocked all literature...
The Rosetta Stone...

A glimpse at what our great works really said...

Forbidden...

Viewing the letter had been known to induce nausea.
Paranoia.

Uttering it caused bleeding of the gums.

I soon became proficient...

Soon after, the institute's Head of Mathematics vanished.
I still own the drill.
Handheld.
Manual...

A trophy?

A keepsake?

A medal....

He was my fifth...

The delicious numeric synchrony still pleases me...

The previous two?

We must not speak of them.

Not yet...

You may be thinking I was a lonely child?

No....

I had 'friends'

I had peers...

Five of us locked in a celestial ballet...

Outsiders?

The first two were my age...we shared an understanding of language...of the inherent power...
We gave the small one a nickname...

Roach...

The second was something of a Romeo...
Obsessed with the magic of sound...

The embrace of future songs.

His name was Johnny....

And then there were the brothers...

The older one fascinated me...such an inherent sense of right and wrong in one so young....

The younger one had a darkness about him...
For a while I considered making him my sixth Cull...

For some reason I did not....

Their names?

Oh....I suspect you will have heard of one of them...
The other maybe not so much....

Lyca....

And

KURT.

Sweet boys....

When I was 14 everything changed.
I discovered my father was less than secure
Faithful.
I found I had a whore spawned brother...
And more...

I saw, for the first time, in my dreams that great screaming hole in Reality...
The aching Void...
The Great Divide...

The Gate of Poets...

And I met a girl....

So very very fair....

Sweet smelling....

Blonde.

And her name was a song....

KATRINA....